D1448610

St Elizabeth's
Children's Hospital

Mills & Boon® Medical™ Romance
welcomes you to
St Elizabeth's Children's Hospital…

Amongst the warmth and heartache,
the laughter and tears, these
medical professionals, devoted to their
young patients, find love and true happiness
where they least expect it…

So come on in and meet them for yourselves!

Look out for more stories set at St Elizabeth's
this month from
Mills & Boon® Medical™ Romance

Jennifer Taylor lives in the north-west of England, in a small village surrounded by some really beautiful countryside. She has written for several different Mills & Boon® series in the past, but it wasn't until she read her first Medical™ Romance that she truly found her niche. She was so captivated by these heart-warming stories that she set out to write them herself!

When she's not writing, or doing research for her latest book, Jennifer's hobbies include reading, gardening, travel, and chatting to friends both on and off-line. She is always delighted to hear from readers, so do visit her website at www.jennifer-taylor.com

Recent titles by the same author:

THEIR BABY SURPRISE*
THE DOCTOR'S BABY BOMBSHELL*
THE GP'S MEANT-TO-BE BRIDE*
MARRYING THE RUNAWAY BRIDE*
THE SURGEON'S FATHERHOOD SURPRISE**

*Dalverston Weddings
**Brides of Penhally Bay

SOMEONE TO TRUST

BY
JENNIFER TAYLOR

 MILLS & BOON®

First published in Great Britain 2000
This edition 2010
Harlequin Mills & Boon Limited,
Eton House, 18-24 Paradise Road, Richmond, Surrey TW9 1SR

ISBN: 978 0 263 21484 0

Harlequin Mills & Boon policy is to use papers that are natural,
renewable and recyclable products and made from wood grown in
sustainable forests. The logging and manufacturing process conform
to the legal environmental regulations of the country of origin.

Printed and bound in Great Britain
by CPI Antony Rowe, Chippenham, Wiltshire

SOMEONE
TO TRUST

CHAPTER ONE

THIS was it. There was no turning back. The first day in a new job. The first day of the rest of her life, in fact. She only hoped it would turn out better than the last year had done!

Karen Young took a deep breath before opening the door. The entrance to St Elizabeth's Children's Hospital was through a glass-enclosed conservatory and she caught a glimpse of herself reflected in one of the many windows as she stepped inside the building. She paused to take stock, needing the reassurance of knowing that she was looking her best.

Moving to London from the small Yorkshire town where she had been born had been a big step and she would be lying if she claimed that she wasn't worried that she might have made a mistake. She had been in London for two days now, barely enough time to get herself settled into the tiny attic flat the letting agency had found for her.

It felt as though her feet hadn't touched the ground for the past month, in fact, as she had worked out her notice and packed her belongings for the move south. It had been a blessing in a way because it had left her little time to brood. It had only been last night, with the time when she would take up her new post fast approaching, that she'd started to have misgivings.

She had left her home and family and everything she knew to come to the city but what if it didn't work out? What if she hated it or, worse still, couldn't cope with the demands of the new job?

By the morning, Karen had worked herself up into such a state of nervous apprehension that she was sure it must show. However, as her worried gaze swept from the top of her immaculately groomed red hair to the tips of her well-polished black shoes she suddenly felt a lot better.

The French plait had been a wise choice, taming her wayward curls and adding a new sophistication to her appearance. A discreet touch of make-up added to the overall picture of a woman in control, the light base coat almost blotting out the sprinkling of freckles across her small straight nose, the subdued bronze lip-gloss subtly highlighting her generously proportioned mouth.

Karen's relieved gaze moved down over the severe lines of her new navy suit. With its slim-fitting skirt and tailored jacket it looked both smart and elegant, its no-nonsense cut just hinting at her trim curves beneath. She had teamed it with a crisp white blouse and low-heeled black shoes and she had to admit that she was pleased with the effect. Smart, businesslike, in control...that was just the image she had wanted to project.

'Excuse me.'

Karen jumped as a deep voice spoke almost in her ear. She glanced round, the colour rushing to her face as she saw the amused smile the man gave her. It was obvious that he knew she had been so busy studying her reflection that she hadn't heard him approaching and she was embarrassed to be caught out like that.

'I'm sorry.' She moved aside to let him pass, turning away so that she wouldn't have to see the amusement in those dark brown eyes again. He walked a few steps across the foyer, then suddenly stopped and swung round.

'Are you all right? You look rather lost. Maybe I can direct you...'

'No!' Karen summoned a smile, aware that her refusal

had been a shade too sharp. She had to stop doing *that*, she berated herself. Had to stop being so defensive all the time. Oh, she understood what was behind it, of course, that it was a legacy from what had happened with Paul. But she shouldn't take her anger out on every good-looking man who spoke to her.

She hurried on, suddenly anxious to extricate herself from the situation with the least fuss possible. Time was marching on and the last thing she wanted was to be late on her first day.

'It's very kind of you but I know where I'm going,' she told him firmly.

'If you're sure?' He gave her a moment to reconsider then shrugged. 'Fine. Have a nice day, then.'

With a last quick smile he continued on his way. Karen's gaze followed him as he strode towards the lifts. He was tall but not overly so, probably around five feet eleven, she'd guess, which was just an inch or so more than her own generous height. He was solidly built, however, with a pair of impressively broad shoulders emphasised by the superb fit of an obviously expensive dark grey suit.

His hair was very thick and black, curling slightly where it touched his collar at the back, but beautifully groomed for all that. Karen frowned as she found herself wondering who he was.

He had spoken with a definite authority which pointed to the fact that he must be on the hospital's staff. However, he didn't remind her of any of the doctors she had met in the past. None of them had worn such expensive clothes, nor had they possessed that air of confidence he had exuded. Oh, a few of the consultants had been like that—assured and self-possessed—but they had been a lot older than he was...

She suddenly realised what she was doing and turned

away, annoyed that she should be wasting time speculating about a stranger. Hurrying across the foyer, she made her way towards the outpatients department, then veered off to the left, following a sign for the speech therapy unit. She felt a small thrill of pleasure as she crossed the empty waiting area and saw the name engraved on a brand-new, shiny brass plate screwed to one of the consulting-room doors: Karen Young. Speech and Language Therapist. Seeing it gave another boost to her confidence. She *had* been right to accept this job! It was time to look to the future instead of brooding about the past any more.

'Karen? Hi! I thought it was you but you were moving at such a rate of knots that I couldn't catch up with you. One of the drawbacks of having such short legs, I'm afraid!'

Karen swung round at the sound of the friendly greeting and smiled as she recognised Denise Roberts, the head of the speech therapy unit. 'Hello, Mrs Roberts. I'm afraid I was so intent on getting here on time that I never saw you,' she explained ruefully.

'First day syndrome?' Denise grinned as she saw Karen's brows rise. She was an attractive, petite woman in her late forties with softly waving fair hair and a friendly smile. Now she used that smile to good effect as she explained.

'I bet you were up at the crack of dawn worrying yourself to death in case the bus didn't turn up. Then there was all the trauma about what to wear!'

Karen laughed as Denise rolled her eyes comically. 'How did you guess?'

'Been there, done that and ended up with the frayed nerves to prove it!' Denise laughed as she unlocked the door to her consulting-room, which was next to the room Karen would be using. Switching on the lights, she turned back and grinned at her.

'Sometimes I wish I were a man because I'm sure they don't spend the amount of time agonising over what to wear that we women do. Anyway, you look great and it's wonderful to see you so sit yourself down and we'll have a cup of coffee.'

Karen chuckled as she followed the older woman into the room. 'I'm sure you're right. Men do have it a lot easier in the fashion stakes!'

She had a sudden mental flash of the man who had stopped and offered to help her, recalling for an instant his casual elegance. She doubted that he wasted time worrying about his appearance. He'd seemed far too sure of himself for that…

'Milk? Sugar?'

Karen jumped as she realised that Denise was speaking to her. She hurriedly pushed all thoughts of the stranger from her mind as she sat by the desk.

'Just milk, please,' she answered, smiling as Denise brought two mugs of instant coffee over and handed her one of them. 'Thanks.'

'Nothing like a fortifying dose of caffeine to start the day.' Denise took an appreciative sip of her coffee then smiled at Karen. 'I was grateful that you could come in today. I know we originally said that you'd be starting on the second of January but I thought it would help if we were able to run through everything without being interrupted all the time. We don't have any appointments scheduled today so it will give us a chance to get sorted out.'

Denise grimaced. 'I hope it didn't ruin your New Year's Eve celebrations, though? Knowing you had to be up bright and early this morning must have put a bit of a damper on things!'

'Not at all. I hadn't anything planned, what with moving and everything.' Karen fixed a bright smile into place, refusing to dwell on how lonely it had felt being on her own when the rest of the country had been celebrating the previous night. She was making a new start and that was what she intended to focus on.

'I don't feel so guilty, then!' Denise laughed. 'Anyway, how are you settling in? It must have been a rush working out your notice and finding somewhere to live down here, especially with Christmas and the new year coming in the middle of it.'

'It was rather but it all worked out in the end. Martyn Lennard gave me the name of a letting agency he recommended and they managed to find me a flat...well, more a bedsit, really.' Karen grimaced as she put her cup on a coaster. 'The addition of a bathroom not even big enough to swing the proverbial cat obviously upgraded the place to flat status!'

'I can imagine! And I bet you're paying a horrendous price for the pleasure of living there?' Denise sighed. 'I love London but the price of property here is no joke. Still, once you get settled in then you'll be able to look round and find something better.'

'That's what I'm hoping. Anyway, it will do for now. It's ample for my needs and the plus side is that it's only a short bus ride away from the hospital,' Karen assured her, not wanting the other woman to think that she was one of those people who were always complaining. As far as she was concerned she had been lucky to find a place to live in the short time she'd had. Now she settled back in her chair and took a long look around the room.

'I like what you've done in here,' she said sincerely. 'It makes the place look less like a hospital consulting-room.'

'That was my intention.' Denise shot a satisfied look at the colourful posters on all the walls, the bright cushions piled on the floor beside a low coffee-table. There was a stack of toys in a big wicker hamper next to it, more toys and books crammed onto shelves nearby. She turned back to Karen with a thoughtful frown.

'Correct me if I'm wrong, but you worked with both adults and children in your last post, didn't you?'

Karen nodded. 'That's right. The hospital where I worked was a general one so both adults and children were referred to me for speech therapy. However, I enjoyed working with the children most of all which is why I applied for this job. I feel so lucky to have got it.'

'It had nothing to do with luck! You were by far the best candidate for the job. We all agreed on that. Even Nick was impressed when he read your CV, and he is *really* choosy when it comes to selecting staff!'

Karen frowned as she tried to place the name. She had been interviewed by a whole panel of people when she had applied for the post. Denise had been there, of course, and Martyn Lennard, the hospital's manager, plus Imogen Drew, the principal nursing officer. The rest of the line-up had been members of the board but she couldn't recall any of them by name.

'Nick?' she queried.

'Bentley. The ENT senior reg,' Denise explained helpfully. 'He was supposed to be there when you were interviewed, standing in for his boss who was on holiday at the time. However, there was some sort of crisis at the last minute so Nick couldn't make it. You certainly wouldn't have forgotten if he had been there!'

She must have realised that Karen didn't understand because she laughed. 'Nick Bentley is the hospital's heartthrob. Think tall, dark, handsome and then some! The fact that Nick is one of the nicest people you could ever meet is simply a bonus.'

Karen laughed dutifully but she could feel her hackles

rising. In her experience handsome men were rarely *nice*! They were so used to getting what they wanted because of their looks that there was no need for them to worry about other people's feelings. This Nick Bentley might have pulled the wool over Denise's eyes but Karen wasn't that gullible. It would take more than good looks to sway her after what she'd been through!

She changed the subject, deeming it wiser to keep her opinions to herself. 'So how about our patients? I take it that I'll be assigned particular children to work with?'

'Yes, that's right. I've been pushing for another therapist for ages. There's certainly enough work to keep us both busy.' Denise grimaced. 'Anyway, I'm sure that I don't have to explain to you, Karen, just how important it is that a child sees the same therapist every time he or she comes for an appointment.'

'No. Gaining a patient's trust is the first major step in being able to help him. It's important when dealing with adults but absolutely vital when working with children,' Karen agreed.

'Exactly.' Denise looked very satisfied with her reply. She opened her mouth to say something else, then stopped as the phone rang. 'Excuse me a moment.'

Karen got up as the other woman answered the call, moving away from the desk to give Denise some privacy. She walked slowly around the room, admiring the posters. Denise had gone to a lot of trouble to collect pictures which would strike a chord in many children and it was an eclectic mix. Posters of pop stars jostled for wall space with favourite cartoon characters!

Karen decided that she would decorate her own room in a similar fashion as soon as possible. Anything that helped stimulate a child to put his feelings into words was worth doing...

'Oh! I...I'll get there somehow! Tell them that I'm on my way!'

Karen glanced round as she heard the anguished note in the other woman's voice. Denise was slumped over her desk and her face was a dreadful shade of grey. It was obvious that something was terribly wrong so Karen hurried over to her.

'What is it? Has something happened? Denise?' She gave the older woman's arm a gentle shake when she didn't answer. Denise took a gulping breath but it was obvious that she was very upset.

'Th-that was my husband. Our son's been involved in an accident. He was driving back to university this morning when there was a pile up on the motorway. Peter's been taken to hospital in Oxford...'

She couldn't go on as a sob welled from her lips. Karen's heart ached as she put her arm around her. 'I'm so sorry, Denise! Is your husband going to drive you to the hospital?'

Denise shook her head. It was hard to understand what she was saying because she was crying so hard. 'John's gone to Leeds on business. He thought it would be quieter driving up there today when most places are closed. They tried to phone us from the hospital and the call got diverted to his mobile number. It will be hours before he can get back here. I just don't know what to do!'

She looked helplessly at Karen, who took a deep breath. This certainly wasn't the time to panic but for the life of her she couldn't think what to suggest. Poor Denise was in no fit state to make her own way to her son's bedside but what was the alternative? She was madly trying to think up a solution when there was a knock on the door and it was thrust open.

'Hi. Has she arrived yet? I thought I'd check her out and see if she lives up to the description...'

The rest of the sentence faded into silence as the new-comer took rapid stock of the situation. Karen barely had time to absorb the fact that it was the man who had offered to help her earlier before he started firing questions at her.

'What's going on? Has something happened?' he demanded, crossing the room in a couple of long strides. 'Is Denise ill?'

Karen took a steadying breath but it had startled her to have him suddenly appear like this. 'Her son has been injured in a car accident. He's been taken to hospital in Oxford. Denise's husband just phoned to tell her the news but he's halfway to Leeds at the moment.'

'And it will take him a couple of hours at least to get back here.'

The man nodded, obviously needing no further explanations to grasp what the problem was. Hunkering down in front of Denise, he took hold of her hands. His tone was so gentle when he spoke to her that Karen felt a lump come to her throat.

'You've got to be very brave, Denise, for Peter's sake. I know it's hard but you have to hang onto the hope that he is going to be all right.'

'I just want to see him...be with him...' Denise took a deep breath, then ran a trembling hand over her face to dry her tears. 'I...I'm sorry about going to pieces like this.'

'It doesn't matter. What matters now is that we get you to the hospital as soon as possible so that you can be with your son.'

The man stood up abruptly but there was infinite gentleness about the way he slid his hand under Denise's arm and helped her to her feet. 'I'll drive you there myself to save time. Come along.'

'Oh, but I couldn't let you do that...' Denise began but he didn't let her finish.

'You can and you will. And I won't take no for an answer!'

He gave Denise a wonderfully warm smile which instantly took the sting out of the words. Karen shifted uncomfortably as a frisson ran down her spine when he turned to include her in it.

She looked away, aware that her heart was beating a shade faster than it had been doing. It had nothing to do with that smile, of course, not one single thing. However, it was harder than it should have been to convince herself of that.

'I'm going to need a little help from you to sort everything out, if you wouldn't mind?'

She firmly focused her thoughts on what was happening as she realised he was addressing her. 'Of course. What would you like me to do?' she asked politely.

His black brows puckered into a frown as he caught the cool note in her voice. However, his tone was perfectly level as he explained what he wanted doing. 'If you could put a call through to Hugh for me and tell him what's happened I'd be grateful. Fortunately, I'm not really due to be here this morning; I just came in because I knew we were short-staffed. But if you could let Hugh know that I'll be back as soon as I can then it would be a great help.'

'Of course. Where will I find him?' she queried, wanting to be sure she got hold of the right person. However, she couldn't help wondering about what he had said.

It was unusual for anyone to come into work out of choice. Most people she knew guarded their precious free time and would have been extremely reluctant to forfeit it without very good reason. It made Karen wonder why he had done so.

Had he been keen to create a good impression, perhaps? It was hard to accept that as the explanation because he didn't strike her as someone who felt the need to impress other people. However, she didn't get a chance to speculate further as he answered her question at that point.

'ENT. He's the consultant there; Hugh Derbyshire. He's probably doing a ward round at the moment so have a word with Sister and she'll pass on the message. Then you'll need to tell Martyn Lennard what's happened and get onto Reception to see if they can cancel Denise's appointments for the next day or so.'

He was urging Denise towards the door while he spoke and was halfway out of the room before Karen realised there was one other vital piece of information she didn't have.

'Wait! You didn't tell me your name.'

He paused to glance back and she felt her heart leap as he treated her to one of those wonderful smiles again. She had the craziest feeling that her temperature actually rose by several degrees and stared at him in bemusement.

'I didn't, did I? Sorry. I'm Nick Bentley, Senior Reg on ENT. I'll see you later anyway. We can introduce ourselves properly then.'

He had gone before Karen could draw breath to answer, although what there was to say she had no idea. She stared at the empty doorway, feeling her heart bouncing around inside her chest.

Nick Bentley. The hospital's heartthrob, or so Denise had called him. Well, so much for her avowals to remain immune to his brand of charm if the way she was acting at the moment was anything to go by!

With a muttered exclamation, Karen picked up the phone. It took some time to inform everyone about what had happened but she was glad to have something to do. At least it kept her mind away from all sorts of other things!

She put the receiver down at last and breathed a sigh of

relief, although it really wasn't the best start to her new job. Denise's absence meant that she was going to be thrown very much onto her own resources in the coming days but she didn't mind that. Being busy was the best antidote possible, she had found. It cured all sorts of ills...

She had a sudden mental picture of Nick Bentley's smiling face before she blocked it from her mind. Nick Bentley *didn't* and *wouldn't* feature in her life so she certainly wasn't going to allow him any leeway in her thoughts! She wasn't fool enough to replace one handsome, smooth-talking charmer with another!

'It's just not good enough! I've better things to do than trail all the way here only to be told that the appointment has been cancelled. I want to speak to whoever's in charge!'

Karen was at her desk the following morning when she heard the sound of angry voices coming from the waiting area. The morning had been hectic despite the fact that Josie, their receptionist, had done her best to cancel Denise's appointments. Inevitably, there had been some people she hadn't been able to get in touch with the previous day and there had been a bit of grumbling when they'd arrived and had to be turned away. However, Karen decided that she couldn't in all conscience leave poor Josie to deal with this problem by herself.

Picking up her jacket, Karen slipped it on before she left the room. She knew from past experience that it was best to present a professional front when dealing with some people and this struck her as one such occasion. She made her way to the reception desk and smiled at the harassed middle-aged woman behind it.

'Can I help, Josie?'

'Please!' Josie gave her a relieved smile. 'I was just explaining to Mr Walters here that Mrs Roberts is unavailable

this morning—' she began before she was rudely interrupted by the heavy-set man standing by the desk.

'I'm not interested in any excuses! I don't know who
you lot think you are. You seem to think you have the right
to do as you please, with no thought for the inconvenience
it causes…'

'It most certainly wasn't like that, Mr Walters.' Karen
raised her voice just enough so that it would carry over the
noise he was making. She carried on when he faltered, not
giving him chance to start haranguing either her or Josie
again.

'Mrs Roberts was called away to a family emergency.
We did our best to contact everyone who had an appointment this morning but, obviously, we were unable to get
in touch with you.'

'I…erm…well, I still don't think it's right!' The man
floundered for a moment, seemingly at a loss to know what
to say next. It was obvious that he wasn't used to anyone
standing up to him the way Karen had done. However, he
soon rallied as he looked at the child standing beside him.
Thrusting the boy forward, he stared belligerently at her.

'It's you lot who keep harping on about how important
it is Kevin has this speech therapy nonsense. To my mind
it's a complete waste of time. The kid's never going to be
able to get the words out without stuttering and stammering
because he's thick!'

Karen took a deep breath. It wouldn't be professional to
tell Mr Walters what she thought of him for saying that but
she was sorely tempted. She glanced at the boy and her
heart went out to him as she saw the misery on his face.
He couldn't have been more than ten years old and she
could imagine the pain it must have caused him if that was
the sort of attitude his father took.

She came to a swift decision, prompted more by a desire

to help the child than to placate his father. 'I'll see Kevin today, Josie. If you could let me have his notes, please?'

'Here they are.' Josie passed a surprisingly slim file across the desk. Her mouth pursed when she saw Karen frown. 'Kevin has only been attending clinic for a few months.'

She shot a speaking look at the boy's father and Karen nodded. She would find out more about the child's background later, although it didn't take a genius to work out that the father must be behind the lack of treatment Kevin had received so far. However, right at that moment she was more concerned with helping the boy as best she could.

She gave him a warm smile. 'My name is Karen Young, Kevin. I'm a speech therapist like Mrs Roberts. Would you like to come along with me and we'll see how well you're doing?'

'Be lucky if he manages to get a word out! Kid's thick as a plank, in my opinion. It's a waste of time, all this nonsense. I've got better things to do than waste a morning hanging around here!'

Mr Walter's irate comments carried after them as Karen led the boy to her room. She didn't look back, not trusting herself not to give the wretched man a piece of her mind. Kevin went and sat in front of the desk as she closed the door on the tirade. He looked such a picture of misery that Karen's heart ached for him. How could any parent be so callous towards his own child?

Picking up the file, she quickly skimmed through the boy's notes. Kevin was eleven years old, the middle child in a family of three boys. He had been first diagnosed as having a speech disorder when he was five and the problem had been picked up during a routine health screening at his school. However, lack of parental co-operation had meant that he hadn't received any therapy until a year previously, and since then his attendance at the clinic had been patchy to say the least.

Karen set aside the notes and smiled at the boy to put him at ease. 'Right, Kevin, why don't you tell me something about yourself? For starters, what's your favourite programme on television?'

Kevin scuffed his feet against the floor and shrugged. Karen gave him a moment but it was obvious that he wasn't going to say anything so she continued in the same friendly fashion.

'Maybe you don't like television all that much. Perhaps you prefer playing football or cricket?'

Once again all she got was a shrug by way of reply. She wasn't deterred nor surprised. Most children who stuttered were reluctant to speak, especially to strangers. The fear of being laughed at was a huge hurdle to overcome and, in Kevin's case, made all the more difficult by his father's lack of understanding.

She got up from the desk and went to her bag. She had brought what she called her 'props' with her that morning, toys and pictures, even some books that she had collected over the years. They had often proved invaluable in breaking down the barriers and encouraging a child to speak. She selected a couple of brightly coloured toy cars and an album of football pictures she had clipped out of magazines, adding almost as an afterthought a beautifully illustrated book on British wildlife.

Returning to her seat, she casually laid the assortment on the desk within Kevin's reach. 'How about a drink of orange squash? I'm really thirsty this morning so I think I'll have one as well.'

She left him sitting there while she went to fetch the drinks from the dispenser in the hallway outside the room. Carefully balancing the two plastic cups of watery squash, she went back and was delighted to see that Kevin had picked up the book and was eagerly turning its pages.

'It's a lovely book, isn't it?' she said lightly as she put their drinks on the desk. 'I love looking through the pictures. Do you like animals? What's your favourite?'

Kevin looked up and his face contorted with the effort it cost him to force out the word. 'B-b-b-b-b-birds!'

'Really?' Karen smiled, delighted that he had managed to get over the first huge hurdle of actually saying something to her. 'Any particular bird or just birds in general?'

He flicked through the glossy pages once more, his face alight with excitement. There was the same struggle once again to get the word he wanted to say out of his mouth but he managed it at last. 'E-e-e-e-eagles!'

'No wonder! They are really magnificent, aren't they?' Karen leant over and studied the photograph Kevin had found. 'I've never seen an eagle except in pictures like this. Have you?'

Kevin shook his head. His eyes were glued to the book as he continued turning the pages. He stopped when he came to one particular photograph which had caught his attention.

'Kestrel,' he announced without the slightest hesitation.

Karen didn't remark on how easily he had managed to say the word but her heart lifted. Opinion was divided on the exact cause of stuttering. Some authorities attributed it to a psychological cause while others were adamant that it was an organic problem. However, both agreed that anxiety made the problem worse. If Kevin gained a little more confidence, then he would be able to relax and learn to deal with it.

'We used to see a lot of kestrels where I lived before,' she told him. 'They were beautiful to watch, so quick and graceful as they swooped over the fields.'

'I...I...' Kevin's face reddened as he struggled to make himself understood. His face twitched and contorted painfully with the effort.

Karen leant over and squeezed his hand. 'Take your time, Kevin. There is no rush.'

He gripped her fingers hard as he tried to follow her advice. She could tell what an effort it was for him but he was obviously determined and she felt very encouraged. The will to overcome any handicap was the best incentive in the world for achieving success.

'I...I w-w-w-w-ish I cou-could see one!'

'Well done!' This time she didn't hide her delight as he managed to say what he wanted to. It was a real achievement and pointed to the fact that therapy would work wonders for him.

Kevin grinned at her, looking like a different child from the dejected boy who had followed her into the room. They carried on for another fifteen minutes, with Karen encouraging him to say what he wanted to. The next time she saw him she would set him some exercises—teach him to give equal emphasis to each syllable, maybe use headphones to relay his speech back to him, both tried and tested methods for those with stutters. However, it was a real breakthrough to have got this far.

Karen took him back to the waiting-room at the end of their session feeling very positive about what they had achieved. His father got up as soon as he saw them. He didn't bother asking how the boy had got on as he came storming over to them.

'And about time too! I'm sick and tired of waiting around this place.'

Karen ignored his rudeness although she could feel her temper rising when she saw that Kevin had that dejected look on his face once more. 'Kevin has done really well today, Mr Walters,' she informed him politely, smiling at the child. 'I'm very pleased with him indeed.'

'Huh! I suppose it depends on what you mean by well.' The man gave an ugly laugh as he looked at the boy. 'You could have a better conversation with a chimp than you can with him! Whole thing's a waste of time but the court says that he has to come here so I can't argue, can I?'

He didn't say anything else as he propelled Kevin towards the exit. Karen closed her eyes and counted to ten but it was impossible to contain her anger.

'Of all the rude, arrogant, horrible people I've ever met that man has to be the worst!'

Her eyes flew open as she heard a soft laugh behind her. Nick Bentley was leaning against the wall and it was obvious that he had witnessed her outburst. Karen flushed as she wondered what he thought. It certainly wasn't the image she had wanted to project—that of the cool, composed professional!

He gave her a slow smile, his eyes dancing with amusement. 'I must make a note of that.'

Karen stared at him in confusion for a moment before she found her voice. 'A note of what?'

'Not to get on the wrong side of you.' He gave another laugh, so deep and vibrant this time that she shivered as she felt the tremors from it ripple down her spine.

'It's a good job that I intend us to be the very best of friends, isn't it, Karen? Otherwise I would be really worried!'

CHAPTER TWO

'WISE man! You certainly don't want to get on the wrong side of Karen, from what I've seen. She put that dreadful man firmly in his place, I can tell you!'

Josie's voice was laced with admiration. She seemed oblivious to the tension but Karen wasn't. She could feel it flowing around her and had to struggle not to let anyone see how disconcerted she felt by what Nick Bentley had said. It hadn't been the actual words; they had been innocuous enough. However, the tone he'd used had added a whole new meaning to them...

She took a deep breath, refusing to let her mind go any further. If Nick Bentley *had* been implying that he was interested in more than just friendship, then it was his hard luck! Once bitten, twice shy was a maxim she firmly believed in.

She gave him a chillingly polite smile. If it had been a well-worn line then she would make sure that he knew how unsuccessful it had been.

'I imagine we shall have to wait and see about that, Dr Bentley. Now, if you will excuse me.'

She made her way back to her office, her grey eyes widening when she went to close the door and found that Nick Bentley had followed her. He came into the room without waiting to be invited, taking the door from her and closing it behind him. There was a quizzical frown on his handsome face as he studied her, a hint of puzzlement in the depths of his liquid-dark eyes.

'If I said something to offend you just now, Karen, then I'm sorry.'

'You didn't!' She heard the defensive note in her voice and turned away, uncomfortable under the searching scrutiny. Moving to her desk, she sat down, using the few seconds it took to give herself breathing space. However, when she looked up she found that Nick was still watching her with the same disturbing intensity.

'Sure?' he persisted softly.

'Of course!' She gave a light laugh, inwardly wincing as she heard the edge it held. It bothered her that he had picked up on her unease so quickly. Since she had found out how Paul had lied to her she had deliberately distanced herself from other people. Never again would she allow anyone to get close enough to hurt her the way Paul had done.

A natural, inbuilt politeness had been honed to the point where it now provided the perfect barrier between herself and the world. Karen had ruthlessly clamped down on the emotional side of her nature as well by learning to curb her quick temper. It had been unusual to let it surface that morning but understandable because she had always found it impossible to ignore abuse in any form whether it concerned an adult or a child. Witnessing how Kevin's father had treated him had opened a chink in her armour, so maybe that was why she had read more into that comment of Nick's than had been intended?

It made sense when she thought about it, enough so that she was able to treat him to a far more natural smile this time. Hopefully, it would allay his suspicions if nothing else. Men like Nick Bentley were so used to women fawning over them that their interest was piqued when they met with any hint of opposition. The last thing she wanted was to become the focus of his attention!

'Sorry. I'm a bit uptight, I expect. Put it down to first week nerves.'

'No wonder!' He gave a rueful laugh as he came and sat on the edge of her desk. Even as Karen watched she could see the curiosity melting from his eyes to leave them full of a warmth and sympathy which touched her despite her determination not to let anything pierce her protective shell again.

'It's been a real baptism of fire, hasn't it? You must be wondering what you've let yourself in for by accepting this job.'

He sighed heavily, his expression momentarily sombre. He really was exceptionally handsome, Karen thought, covertly studying the perfectly chiselled cheek-bones and jaw, the sensuous curve of his lips.

He bent forward to pick up one of the toy cars she had got out for Kevin and she caught the elusive drift of some expensive cologne. She sniffed appreciatively, savouring the tangy aroma, before she realised what she was doing.

'How was Denise's son?' she asked, getting up abruptly to gather together the rest of her props because it seemed wiser not to sit there and let her mind run riot the way it seemed to be doing.

'Holding his own...just!' Nick grimaced as he ran the toy car across the blotter. 'He's got two fractured legs and some internal damage. They were just taking him up to theatre when we got there.'

'Was Denise able to speak to him?' Karen asked, forgetting her own problems as she thought about what the poor woman must be going through.

'Yes. He was conscious, so that was something at least. And knowing that his mother was there will have been a comfort to him as well.' Nick picked up the car and tossed it in the palm of one large, well-shaped hand. 'I wish I could have stayed with her but I had to get back here.'

'I'm sure Denise was grateful for what you did,' Karen said quickly, wondering why she felt this need to reassure him. She hurried on, not wanting to examine her motives in any depth. 'Denise was so upset when she got that call and I had no idea what to suggest for the best.'

'I'm sure you would have thought of something pretty quickly. From what Josie was saying just now, you are pretty resourceful.'

He gave her a lazy smile as he got up and came over to where she was standing. Reaching past her, he neatly placed the toy car on the shelf next to the others. Karen's breath caught as she felt his arm brush hers. She moved away at once, putting several feet between them because she was more disturbed by the contact than she had any right to be.

She wasn't interested in handsome men—in *any* man, in fact! She had learned her lesson the hard way and never again would she be foolish enough to trust a man or believe his lies. Men were incapable of being truthful, in her opinion. It wasn't part of their make-up. But she understood that now and wasn't going to make the same mistake that she had made with Paul.

'I don't know about that,' she said with forced lightness to disguise how on edge she felt once again. 'However, if there is one thing I can't abide it's a bully and that's what Kevin's father is.'

'Denise mentioned something about him when the boy came for his last appointment.' Nick frowned. 'Evidently, he said some very derogatory things about the child. She was most annoyed, as I recall.'

'I can imagine. I couldn't believe it when he stated quite openly that he thought his son was stupid!' Karen took a deep breath as she felt a renewed surge of anger on the child's behalf. It wouldn't achieve anything to let her feelings get the better of her so she must stay calm.

'People like that shouldn't have kids,' Nick observed in disgust. 'If your parents don't believe in you, then who will?'

'Exactly.' Karen couldn't help agreeing with him. 'If my mother and father hadn't believed in me then I wouldn't be here today.'

'What do you mean?'

There was no mistaking the interest in his voice. Karen experienced a momentary qualm but there didn't seem any harm in explaining.

'I had great difficulty learning to read and write when I started school. However, my parents always had faith in me and sought the best help they could find.' She shrugged. 'It turned out that I am dyslexic and that was what was causing the problem.'

He whistled softly. 'Really? Obviously you've managed to overcome your difficulties otherwise you wouldn't be able to do this job. You need to be a graduate to train for speech therapy, I believe?'

'That's right. I studied English and Linguistics at university then did a two-year post graduate course at Sheffield,' she explained.

'What made you decide on this as a career, though?' Nick asked thoughtfully.

She sighed softly, her face clouding for a moment. 'My father had a stroke in my last year at university. His speech was badly affected and he was dreadfully embarrassed by the fact that he couldn't make himself understood.'

'And you saw the benefit he gained from speech therapy?' Nick was ahead of her again, piecing together the few facts she had told him with such little difficulty that

Karen felt uneasy once more. How did he manage to latch into her thoughts so readily?

She shrugged, instinctively retreating behind her defensive shield once again. 'Something like that,' she agreed coolly.

He didn't appear deterred as she had hoped he would be. 'I'm sure that was the reason, Karen. We're all influenced one way or another by circumstances.'

There was a note in his voice which immediately aroused her curiosity although she knew it wasn't wise. She should be keeping him at arm's length rather than asking questions but she couldn't resist finding out what he had meant.

'That sounds as though you're speaking from the heart?' she queried softly.

'I am.' He smiled but his eyes were sad. 'I'd just finished my stint as a junior houseman when my older brother, Ed, was killed in a skiing accident. We were very close and his death hit me hard. What made it worse was that his wife was expecting their first child at the time.'

'Oh, how awful!' Karen exclaimed, her sympathies instantly aroused. 'It must have been a dreadful time for you all.'

'It was.' He sighed as he ran his fingers through his thick black hair causing a heavy lock to fall onto his forehead. Karen felt a little fluttering sensation in the pit of her stomach and looked away, shocked by the desire she felt to smooth the shiny black strand into place. It was a moment before she realised that Nick had carried on speaking.

'The baby was fine when he was born. Then when he was six months old he contracted meningitis. It was an awful time for Melanie, as you can imagine. It was touch and go whether Jamie would pull through. Fortunately, he did. However, it wasn't long before Mel realised there was something wrong with him.'

Nick went to the window and looked out. Karen had the feeling that he didn't want her to see his expression at that moment but she could hear from the tone of his voice how the memory still grieved him.

'Tests subsequently showed that Jamie was severely deaf as a result of the meningitis.' He shrugged but she could see the regret on his face as he looked round. 'He's five now and a great little chap but seeing what Melanie has been through with him is what set me on my present course. If I can do something to help kids like Jamie, then that's all I ask.'

'I can understand that,' Karen said softly, touched by what he had told her. 'You must be very fond of him?'

'I am.' Nick came back to the desk. 'I suppose in a way I've tried to make up for the fact that he hasn't got a father. It's what Ed would have wanted me to do, I'm sure.'

Karen didn't say anything although she couldn't help wondering if Nick's concern encompassed his sister-in-law as well. The phone suddenly rang and she picked up the receiver, not at all sorry to have something to take her mind off that last thought. Nick Bentley's relationship with his sister-in-law certainly wasn't her business!

It was a relief when Josie announced that her next appointment had arrived and was waiting outside. Perhaps it would be wiser to put a stop to this exchange of confidences before it got out of hand, she decided as she hung up. She was willing to foster an amicable working relationship with Nick Bentley, but that was as far as it went.

'My next appointment is here,' she told him briskly in a tone which was meant to bring the impromptu meeting to a close.

'And I'd better go and find Hugh before he thinks I've deserted him.' Nick sketched her a wave as he headed for the door. Karen turned towards her desk then jumped when he suddenly popped his head round the door again.

'Oh, I'll be seeing you later. Around three. Bye for now.'

He didn't give her chance to reply as he hurried away. Karen went to the door and got there just in time to see him disappearing into the lift. She frowned as her mind anxiously raced through a list of possible reasons why Nick should need to see her that afternoon before she realised how silly she was being.

What difference did it make? Nick Bentley was a colleague. That was all.

'Good! That was excellent, Jessica. Well done!'

Karen smiled at the little girl and received a shy smile in return. Jessica Price was her last patient before lunch and she was pleased with the progress the five-year-old had made. Now she turned to Jessica's mother as the little girl picked up a brightly coloured rag doll and began plaiting its hair.

'She's coming on really well, Mrs Price. I can see from Jessica's notes that you are keen to take an active part in helping her overcome her problems and it's obvious that you have been working hard with her.'

Hilary Price smiled with pleasure. A rather plain woman in her late thirties, she was obviously devoted to her small daughter. 'We do some of the exercises Mrs Roberts showed us each day, before and after school.'

'Excellent! And they are obviously paying dividends. Jessica's speech is improving nicely.'

Karen checked the child's notes again. Little Jessica had difficulty speaking although IQ tests pointed to the fact that she was above average intelligence. There was no physical reason for the problem, either, so a series of exercises had been devised to help the child develop her language skills.

'You're still doing the tissue exercise?' Karen looked up with a smile. 'I know it seems funny in these high-tech times but it's very effective!'

Hilary Price laughed. 'It's Jessica's favourite! Practising her p's and b's is the first thing we do each morning. Oh, look, she's showing you how well she can do it.'

Karen laughed as she saw that the little girl had taken a paper tissue from her pocket and was holding it close to her lips. Each time Jessica managed to say the letter 'p' properly the tissue was puffed outward. However, when she said the letter 'b' the tissue didn't move. The exercise, while extremely simple, would help enormously to clarify her speech.

'That's great, Jessica! Clever girl,' Karen praised, earning herself another shy smile. She turned to the child's mother once again.

'I know how time-consuming it can be practising individual letters but it's very worthwhile. Once Jessica learns to say each letter clearly then fluent speech will be that much easier for her.'

'That's what I'm hoping.' Hilary lowered her voice but there was real pain in her eyes as she glanced at her daughter. 'It breaks my heart to see how upset and frustrated she gets when she can't make herself understood. And since she started school this September it's got so much worse.'

'Other children can be very cruel, can't they?' Karen agreed softly. 'I imagine that Jessica is finding it hard to fit in when she can't communicate properly.'

'She is.' A tear trickled down Hilary's cheek. 'The other children won't play with Jessica, you see. I was so worried about her that I went to the school one lunch-time to see how she was and found her standing on her own in the playground. When I spoke to her teacher about it, though, she was most unsympathetic.'

Karen bit back a sigh because it was a story she had heard all too often. Pressure of work often meant that teachers found it hard to give a child the extra help needed. 'Then we shall just have to work even harder, won't we? I'm quite sure that Jessica can overcome this problem with time and patience.'

'That's what I'm hoping.' Hilary Price stood and offered Karen her hand with a sweet smile. 'Thank you, Miss Young. I'm sure that Jessica is going to flourish under your guidance.'

Karen smiled to herself as the pair left the room. It was a very satisfying feeling being able to help someone, especially when that person was a child. She was suddenly convinced that the move to London had been the right thing to do.

On that upbeat thought she locked her office and went for her lunch. It was a little daunting entering the bustling canteen on her own. She hadn't bothered with lunch the previous day, preferring to carry on working at her desk. Denise's absence had meant that she'd had to read through the notes on the various cases she would be dealing with herself and she hadn't wanted to miss anything. However, she was too hungry to ignore the grumblings of her tummy today.

The food looked delicious, though, so that it was hard to choose from the selection on offer. In the end Karen opted for a portion of lasagne with a side salad and a glass of fresh orange juice. She paid at the till, then looked round for somewhere to sit, but every seat seemed to be taken.

'Over there by the window. Here, let me take that and I'll lead the way.'

Karen barely had time to register what was happening before Nick Bentley had lifted the tray out of her hands and started across the canteen. She opened her mouth to explain that she had no intention of joining him, only he was too far away to hear without her having to raise her voice. The thought of causing a scene was more than Karen could bear so she trailed after him, inwardly fuming about his high-handedness.

'Right, here we are.' Nick had put her tray on a table by the window and was waiting for her to catch him up. He frowned as he caught sight of her mutinous expression. 'Is something wrong, Karen?'

'Yes. I would prefer it if you didn't—'

'So you're Karen, are you? Nick's been singing your praises so it's good to meet you at last!'

Her angry words dried up as a man rose from a seat at the next table and smiled at her. He was several years older than Nick, with closely cropped steel-grey hair and a friendly smile. When he offered her his hand, Karen automatically took it.

'I'm Hugh Derbyshire,' he explained. 'Nick's so-called boss, only I prefer to think of myself as the leader of our little team. And this is Andrew Lee, our junior registrar, and Eleanor Davidson, who has just joined us as our new houseman.'

Karen smiled at the others. 'Nice to meet you all.'

There was a chorus of greetings before Hugh checked his watch. 'Right, gang, time we were on our way. Duty calls and all that.' He glanced at Nick. 'I'll see you later for the team meeting. OK?'

Nick nodded. He waited until the others had left before taking his seat. He looked up in surprise when he realised that Karen was making no attempt to sit down. 'If you don't hurry up your lunch is going to be cold.'

Karen was sorely tempted to tell him that she was no longer hungry only her stomach chose that moment to rumble loudly. She sat down abruptly, feeling annoyed and on edge at being put in such an awkward position.

She didn't want to have lunch with Nick Bentley! She didn't want to have anything to do with him which wasn't directly connected with their work.

'Look, I'm sorry. Obviously, I made a mistake commandeering you like that. If you want me to leave you in peace then just say the word and I'll disappear.'

Karen flushed as she heard the wryness in his voice. It immediately brought it home to her how silly she was being. What harm could there be in two colleagues having lunch together, after all?

'No, it's me who should apologise. It was kind of you to find me a place to sit. It's really busy in here today.'

She picked up her knife and fork, determined to act as naturally as possible. Would she have been so wary if it had been Hugh Derbyshire seated across the table? a small voice whispered before she feigned strategic deafness. Thoughts like that certainly wouldn't help!

'It is, but then it's busy in here every day. Forget all those horror stories you hear about canteen fare. This place should be Michelin rated!'

Nick accepted her apology with easy grace although she wasn't blind to the curiosity in his eyes when she happened to glance up. She hurriedly focused her attention on her meal, her elegant brows rising as she took her first mouthful of the lasagne.

'Why, it's delicious!' she said in amazement and heard him laugh softly.

'I can see you didn't believe me.' He gave her a lazy grin as he forked up some of his own chili and rice. 'Obviously, you're a woman who prefers to make up her own mind rather than rely on other people's opinions, Karen.'

The warmth in his voice turned the remark into a compliment and Karen felt her heartbeat quicken. She didn't say anything, however, pretending that she was too busy eating to speak. Nevertheless, she sensed that Nick was aware that it was just a ruse. It disconcerted her that he should be able to see through her so easily. Most people found her politeness a barrier, but, obviously, he didn't.

They ate in silence for a few minutes, each of them busy with their own thoughts, although when she chanced a glance at Nick there was nothing on his face to indicate that his thoughts were anywhere near as uncomfortable as hers were!

The thought was so unsettling that she made up her mind to take control before the situation became even more complicated. Nick Bentley was a very astute man but that was all he was. He wasn't omnipotent! He couldn't affect her in any way if she chose not to let him.

She put her knife and fork neatly on her plate as she finished the last mouthful of lasagne. 'That was delicious. And I shall certainly eat here again if the food is always this good.'

'It is. As you'll find out.' Nick treated her to a smile as he sat back in his chair. Looping one arm casually around the back of it, he picked up his cup. 'It's one of the perks of working here at Lizzie's, but then there are so many others that you soon realise how privileged you are to be part of the team.'

Karen was surprised by that. In her experience men like Nick Bentley usually held such high opinions of themselves that they felt they were doing everyone a favour by working in a place. She couldn't help questioning what he had said.

'Surely it's the hospital which reaps the benefits of your expertise?'

She hadn't intended to let that note of scepticism slip in

but she could hear it all the same. Nick obviously heard it as well because he frowned.

'It's a two-way street, I suppose. Lizzie's certainly couldn't function without its staff and we need jobs.' He shrugged but there was no doubting that he was telling the truth. 'However, I'm very conscious of how much I have gained both personally and professionally through working here. The staff in this hospital are all totally dedicated to their work and give one hundred per cent commitment. However, when you see what some of these kids we treat have to go through then you realise how lucky you are.'

Karen looked down at her glass, feeling strangely moved by what he had said. Paul had worked with children as well, funnily enough. He had been a junior registrar on the children's ward with ambitions to move as high as he could up the ladder in that field. However, Paul had never really *felt* anything for the children in his care and had certainly never empathised with them or their parents.

It made her realise that not all doctors were like Paul, that some, like Nick Bentley, saw their young patients as children first and *cases* second. Somehow, realising that pushed everything slightly out of sync and it alarmed her. She didn't want to have to adjust her opinion of men in general and certainly not of one man in particular. Something warned her it would be a mistake.

She pushed back her chair so fast that its legs scraped on the tiles. She saw a couple of people turn to look her way and coloured. It made her realise how out of character she was behaving and that it had to stop. Cool, calm and composed...funny how hard it was all of a sudden to achieve that state.

'I'd better get back,' she stated as calmly as she could. 'I want to check through my notes for this afternoon's list.'

'Of course. It's a shame that Denise can't be there to run

through everything with you but I'm sure you will cope admirably, Karen.'

There was an equally cool note in Nick's voice which made her look sharply at him. However, the smile he gave her was too bland to discern much from it. If he had been teasing her then there was no *proof*...

'I hope so.' She treated him to a deliberately bright smile, not letting herself dwell on it. The thought that Nick might have guessed that her composure was all a façade was too unsettling.

He pushed back his own chair and stood. 'I'd better make tracks as well and catch up with Hugh. We'll see you later for the team meeting.'

'Team meeting?' she echoed uncertainly.

'Uh-huh.' He grinned as he saw her confusion. 'Monday afternoons we meet up to talk through our case load and Denise usually tries to be there. With her being absent, you'll be standing in for her. ENT sends a number of patients for speech therapy, as you know, and Hugh is really keen that we all work together.'

'I...I see.' Karen struggled to digest this but it was obvious that she would be seeing rather more of Nick Bentley than she had anticipated.

A ripple ran down her spine, like a cool finger, and she shivered at the thought. Taking a firmer grip on her tray, she treated him to her most distant smile, the one which said clearly, 'Keep Away!'

'Then I shall see you later, Dr Bentley.'

'Oh, you will, you most certainly will.'

He picked up his dishes and headed across the canteen, pausing only long enough to stack his tray in the rack by the door. Karen counted to ten, then added another ten for good luck but it didn't achieve much. No matter how hard she tried to convince herself that had been just a casual remark, it didn't work!

'See you've succumbed as well.'

Karen looked round as she realised that someone was speaking to her. She summoned a smile as she spotted Josie crammed into a narrow gap on a nearby table. 'Sorry, I'm not with you?'

The receptionist laughed as she shared a conspiratorial look with the other women on her table. 'She's pretending she doesn't understand but we can see right through her, can't we, girls?'

There was a chorus of laughing agreements from the group. However, Karen still had no idea what they were talking about and it obviously showed. Josie sighed theatrically.

'You're suffering from the same affliction we all are: Bentley fever. That man could turn any woman's head!'

Karen dredged up a smile as the whole group dissolved into laughter. 'Oh, I think I'm immune.'

Josie wiped her streaming eyes with a tissue. 'That's what they all claim! But you tell me that again in a couple of months' time and *then* I'll believe you!'

The sound of their laughter followed Karen as she made for the door. She paused to deposit her tray, then rushed outside. It was quiet in the corridor and she stopped to draw breath, needing to get herself under control again. However, it was difficult...very difficult indeed.

Her heart was pounding, her pulse was racing, her blood pressure almost at explosive levels. She closed her eyes and tried to collect herself but that was a mistake. The image of Nick Bentley's handsome face which conjured itself up like a genie escaping from a bottle certainly didn't soothe her shattered nerves!

Karen groaned as her eyes flew open. Was she a woman

or a mouse? Was she really so...so spineless that she couldn't deal with this in a rational way?

Nick Bentley was attractive and charming and dedicated to his job but he was also a *man* and men were strictly off limits as far as she was concerned.

Easy. Simple. It was as straightforward as that. *Ergo* she had nothing whatsoever to worry about!

Oh, yeah? her conscience jeered as she pressed the button to summon the lift. Then why was she getting herself into such a lather?

'Oh, shut up!' she exclaimed, then flushed when she discovered that there were other people behind her waiting for the lift. Nobody said anything but she was glad when she was able to flee back to the sanctuary of her office and shut the door.

She went to the window and stared across the leafy green vista of nearby Regent's Park. It was only the second day in her new job and already so much had happened. Now she had the afternoon to look forward to. Heaven alone knew what that would bring!

CHAPTER THREE

'SO THAT brings us to the end of the list you have there. However, there is one other case I want to discuss if you wouldn't mind hanging on a few minutes longer.'

Hugh Derbyshire smiled round at the group assembled in his office that afternoon. It had been a fascinating hour and Karen had learned a lot as they had discussed the various cases she would be involved with. Team work was all important at St Elizabeth's and her role was considered as vital to the children's eventual recovery as everyone else's.

She had to admit that she was impressed by the dedication everyone had shown, and that it had been easier than she had expected to accept Nick Bentley's presence when she had been concentrating on work. Now she looked up as he spoke and it was impossible to miss the puzzlement in his voice.

'Another case? How come?' A frown darkened his brow as he checked the printed list which Hugh had handed round before the meeting.

'As I said, it isn't on the list because I've only just heard that we have the go-ahead for the operation.'

Hugh smiled as Nick's head shot up. Karen looked from one to the other, wondering what was going on. The atmosphere was electric all of a sudden yet she couldn't understand what had caused it.

'You don't mean...?' Nick stopped and she saw him swallow convulsively. It was obvious that he was deeply affected by what was happening and Karen felt her own nerves tighten in response to the signals he was giving out. It shocked her that she should feel this way.

She didn't *want* to empathise with Nick Bentley! She didn't want to regard him as anything more than a col- league. Yet she couldn't deny that she, too, was holding her breath as she waited for Hugh to reply.

'I do. I've been told that your nephew's operation can go ahead. It will be scheduled for the beginning of next week.' Hugh laughed as he heard Nick gasp. 'I was tipped off by Martyn Lennard that we should get permission soon but I didn't want to raise your hopes until I had actual confirmation.'

'I should have realised you had something up your sleeve...!' Nick shook his head but it was obvious to every- one how moved he was by the news.

He stood and offered Hugh his hand and there was a note in his voice which brought a lump to Karen's throat. 'Thanks, Hugh. I can't tell you what this means to me. Mel will be thrilled when she finds out.'

'I already phoned her.' The consultant smiled broadly as he shook Nick's hand. 'She was thrilled to bits and wanted to phone you right away but I persuaded her to let me make the announcement. There was no way I was letting that beautiful sister-in-law of yours steal my thunder!'

Everyone laughed at the smugness in Hugh's voice. However, Karen couldn't stop her mind from spinning off at a tangent. So Melanie Bentley was beautiful, was she? Why didn't that surprise her?

She dragged her thoughts back to what was happening as Nick turned to her with a wry smile. 'You must think we're all crazy, Karen, but we've been waiting for this for what seems like ages. I've prayed night after night that Jamie could have a cochlear implant and at long last it's actually going to happen.'

It was impossible not to be touched by his delight. Karen found herself responding to it without any of her usual reserve. 'Then it must be wonderful news for you.'

'It is! And it's all thanks to Hugh,' Nick declared, turning to his boss.

'If anyone should take the credit, then it's you,' Hugh replied firmly, refusing to accept all the kudos. 'You've never given up even when the odds were stacked against you.'

'What do you mean?' Karen asked, her curiosity piqued.

'Well, before a child can be offered a cochlear implant we have to be sure it will be of value to him. I'm not sure how much you know about the implant but it works by receiving and passing on electrical signals to the brain,' Nick explained. 'One or more tiny electrodes are implanted either inside or outside the cochlea, which is the organ in the ear which turns sound vibrations into nerve impulses.

'A miniature receiver is also fitted under the skin—usually behind the ear—at the same time, with a wire connecting it to the electrodes. However, when a child has become deaf as a result of meningitis there can be a problem if new bone has formed in the cochlea.'

'I see. But, obviously, tests have shown that your nephew's operation is viable?' Karen said softly.

'Yes. However, we've had to wait a few months until we got funding. There are just too many children needing the operation and not enough money to go round, I'm afraid.' Nick's tone was even but that didn't mean Karen couldn't tell how angry he was about the situation.

'So your nephew was on a waiting list of children needing cochlear implants?' she guessed.

'Yes. It's been so frustrating because everyone agrees that, the earlier a child has the implant, the greater the benefit he will derive from it. I don't need to tell you how vital it is for a child to learn to communicate clearly and for a deaf child that is a major hurdle.'

'Then it's no wonder that you are so thrilled,' Karen declared, finding it impossible to remain detached in the face of his enthusiasm.

'I am!' Nick's grin was so infectious that Karen found herself smiling back at him. It was only when everyone got up to leave that she realised they had been smiling inanely at one another for several seconds.

She turned away, making a great production of stowing her notes into her case. She left Hugh's office and went straight back to her own department where she was kept busy for the rest of the afternoon. She didn't see Nick again that day and she was glad. He had a very unsettling effect on her, one way or another.

'Right, Becky. Now we are going to practise words beginning with the letter "m".'

Karen smiled as nine-year-old Rebecca Dobbs groaned. It was mid-morning and Becky was her second patient of the day. So far things had gone smoothly even though Denise had rung to say that she wouldn't be in for the rest of the week.

Josie had managed to get in touch with all Denise's patients for that morning and was working her way through the rest of the week's list. Karen was hopeful that the day would go without any major hitches and so far there was nothing to suggest that it wouldn't.

'I know you probably hate this part of the session but it will help. Promise!' she assured the child.

'That's what grown-ups say when they want you to do something boring!' Becky glowered her displeasure but Karen wasn't deterred.

Becky had been born with a cleft lip and palate which

had been repaired with a series of operations. Now there was little visible sign of the child's birth defect but there was still some evidence of it in her rather nasal speech. Although Becky might hate the exercises, Karen knew that she would be glad she had done them in years to come.

'OK, then, I'll strike a bargain with you. You do the exercises for me and then I'll let you have a little treat for the last ten minutes.'

'What sort of treat?' Becky demanded but Karen shook her head.

'You'll just have to wait and see. Is it a deal or not?'

Becky hesitated, obviously unsure whether to accept the offer or not. However, in the end she sighed. 'S'ppose so.'

'Good. Now first I want you to read these simple words for me, then we'll try some really difficult ones!'

Becky groaned as she picked up the printed card. 'It's just like when I was a baby...' She set off down the list with Karen gently correcting her whenever the sound was slightly off-key.

Treating a child with a severely cleft palate and lip required a team of experts. Apart from surgery to close the gap in the roof of her mouth and the split in her upper lip, Becky had needed extensive dental and orthodontic treatment as well.

Producing recognisable speech involved air being passed through the vocal cords and then being shaped by movements of the lips, tongue, lower jaw and soft palate, and that was where Karen's input began. She was very aware of being part of the team which had invested so much time and effort into Becky's future and was determined to do the best that she could for the child.

Patiently, she took Becky through the list, paying particular attention to those sounds she had the greatest difficulty with such as the letters 'm' and 'n'.

'That was excellent, Becky. Well done!' she praised when she sensed that the little girl was getting bored. Most children had a low boredom threshold and she had learned by experience to move on to something else as soon as they started to lose interest.

She picked up another reading card, in the form of a cartoon strip this time. Each picture was accompanied by a short sentence designed to make a child work hard at articulating particular sounds. It was one of a series Karen had designed and drawn herself and she knew how effective it could be, although most children just thought it was a bit of fun reading a cartoon rather than a page from a book.

She handed it to Becky and smiled as she heard the child giggle as she looked at the cartoon pictures of a little boy and his pet lamb. 'Now, can you read this for me, sweetheart? Then we shall have some fun!'

Becky eagerly read out the sentences, repeating several of the words with good grace when Karen asked her to.

'That was great, Becky! Now you just sit there while I get everything set up.'

Karen went to the cupboard and lifted out the machine she had discovered tucked away in the back of it that morning. She had been thrilled to see it as she knew that she could put it to good use.

'What is it?' Becky demanded, getting up to have a look at what Karen was doing. She frowned as she tried to read the inscription on the side of the machine. 'Kar...kara...'

'Karaoke. It's a machine that plays music while you sing along. Want to have a go?'

'Yes, please!' Becky clapped her hands with delight.

Karen sorted through the accompanying song sheets and found one she thought the child might know. It took her a few minutes to get everything ready and Becky was a little hesitant at first when it actually came to singing to the music.

Karen joined in to encourage her, smiling as Becky quickly overcame her embarrassment. Music was a great leveller with children like this, she had found. Often a child with a debilitating stutter could sing without pause while those barely able to form a coherent word could often be persuaded to try that bit harder to make some sort of sound. As she heard Becky singing her little heart out, her own voice lifted in sheer joy, sounding clear and sweet as it rang around the room.

The music came to an end. Karen got up to select another track for the little girl to sing then swung round as she heard the sound of applause. Nick Bentley was standing by the door and it was obvious from his expression that he had enjoyed their impromptu recital.

'That was great. You two could sell tickets singing like that!' He included Becky in the compliment, smiling as the little girl laughed with delight.

'It was fun! Can we do another one, Karen...please?'

'Well, I'm not sure...' Karen hesitated, although she had been intending to let Becky have another turn seeing as the first had been such a success. However, the fact that Nick was in the room was a little inhibiting. She felt deeply self-conscious at the thought of him listening while she had sung her heart out.

'Don't let me stop you,' he said immediately, making her feel more self-conscious than ever as she realised that he had guessed what was behind her reluctance. Did the wretched man have second sight or something? she thought with a spurt of irritation.

'You aren't!' she snapped, then quickly modified her tone when she saw him blink. 'I mean, I'm sure you must be in a rush. Did you want to see me about something?'

'It can wait. I hadn't realised you were busy or I wouldn't have interrupted. But I heard the music and couldn't resist popping in to see what was happening.'

He winked conspiratorially at Becky. 'I bet if you ask Karen nicely she'll let you have another turn once I've gone.'

'Will you, Karen? Please?'

'Yes, all right,' Karen agreed as Nick left the room. However, her mind was only partly on what she was doing as she selected another track and found the song sheet that went with it. She didn't join in this time, using the excuse that she wanted to record Becky's singing so that she could take the tape home for her parents to hear. However, she knew it was an excuse. Nick's unexpected appearance had thrown her off balance once again.

What was it about him that got to her like this?

Was it simply because he was a *man* and she didn't trust men?

Karen sighed as the music came to an end and she re-wound the tape. If only it were that simple, but there was no point lying to herself. She'd had no problem relating to Hugh Derbyshire or any of the other men she had met so far. It was just Nick who seemed to irritate and upset her, Nick who made her feel so...well, so *aware* of him.

She grimaced as she realised how much time she had spent thinking about him in the past few days. She must make up her mind to put all thoughts of Nick Bentley out of her head...and keep them out!

It was another busy morning and Karen was ready for a break by the time lunch-time arrived. However, recalling what had happened the previous day, she decided it might be wiser to give the canteen a miss. Bumping into Nick again was something she wanted to avoid.

It was a lovely, crisp sunny day so she decided to go for a walk in the park. There was a mini shopping mall in the hospital's foyer so she stopped to buy herself something to eat on her way out. She went to Dunwoody, the fruit and flower shop, and bought a couple of apples and a carton of yoghurt from the small grocery section.

Karen paid for her purchases then left the building, content in the knowledge that she wasn't going to starve even if her lunch wouldn't be as filling as the previous day's had been. Still, if it meant avoiding Nick Bentley then that was a definite plus factor in her view!

'Hi, there! Decided to make the most of this glorious weather while it lasts?'

Karen spun round so fast that one of the apples flew out of her hands. Nick handed it back to her, a frown darkening his brow as he saw the expression on her face.

'Hey, are you all right?' he asked in obvious concern.

'Fine,' she snapped. 'You startled me, that's all. Do you always creep up on people like that?'

'I wasn't aware that I had crept up on you. Sorry.'

He treated her to an amused smile and Karen felt her face heat as she realised that her reaction had been way over the top. She set off in the direction of the park as fast as her long legs would carry her, hoping that Nick would take the hint that she didn't want any company. However, it was a vain hope, it appeared.

He loped along beside her, his hands thrust into the pockets of his trousers as though he hadn't a care in the world. It was a mild day for the time of year and he hadn't bothered to put a top coat over his dark grey suit. His jacket blew open as he walked, the breeze flattening his pale blue shirt against his muscular chest.

Karen felt her pulse perform the most peculiar manoeuvre as she glanced at him—a kind of blip almost like a hiccup. It annoyed her intensely. So Nick Bentley *was* an extremely handsome man and many women would find him attractive. However, she was immune to *any* man's attractions and that included his. The sooner he realised that, the better it would be for everyone concerned!

She stopped dead and glared at him. 'Are you following me?'

'That depends where you're going, I suppose.' He gave her a friendly smile, quite unperturbed by the frosty note in her voice. '*I'm* going to the park. Where are you going?'

'I *was* going to the park,' she stated pointedly.

He shrugged. 'Then we may as well walk over there together.'

He carried on, leaving Karen in something of a quandary. She really didn't want to go with him yet the alternative— turning tail and going back to the hospital—held even less appeal. She would be damned if she'd let him think that she was at all bothered about being with him...even if it was true!

She soon caught him up, returning his smile with an equally bland one. She had a feeling that Nick knew how uneasy she was around him but she refused to give him any proof. He couldn't affect her if she didn't let him, she reminded herself. However, she made up her mind that she would make her escape as soon as she could just to err on the safe side.

Nick pointed towards the lake as they entered the park by one of the side gates. 'There's a tea stall over there where I usually buy myself a sandwich. Why don't we head in that direction?'

Karen shook her head. 'Look, Dr Bentley, I don't want to be rude but...'

'But you'd prefer it if I took a long walk off a short pier, metaphorically speaking, of course?' He laughed softly when she made no attempt to deny it. 'Mmm, in the interest of inter-departmental harmony, then maybe you are wise not to answer that. However, there was something I'd like to speak to you about if you could spare me a few minutes.'

'Work, do you mean?' she queried, not sure that she enjoyed being teased like that. It hinted at an intimacy that she certainly didn't intend to encourage.

'Yes. I know this is your lunch-break and you're well within your rights to refuse. But I really would appreciate your advice.'

Karen hesitated a moment more before making up her mind. After all, what harm could there be in them talking about a work-related topic? The last thing she wanted was to earn herself a reputation of being uncooperative when she'd only just started in the job.

'All right,' she agreed evenly. 'I'd be happy to help any way I can.'

'Great. I really appreciate this, Karen.'

He gave her a warm smile, then set off along the path. There were quite a few people about with it being such a wonderfully sunny day, mainly young women with children in tow. Karen couldn't help noticing the interested glances being cast Nick's way as they crossed the park. He was so handsome, of course, that it was little wonder he attracted attention from the opposite sex, although he appeared quite oblivious to it.

Unless he was just so *used* to women drooling over him that he accepted it as his due, Karen thought cynically, recalling the impact Paul had made on the opposite sex. Paul had only needed to enter a room for all female eyes to focus on him. It was one of the reasons why she had been so reluctant to go out with him at first.

She hadn't believed that he could have been serious about wanting to take her out when he could have had his pick of any number of women, but slowly, persistently, he had worn her down. It had only been later—much, much later—that she had discovered what a fool she had been.

'Karen?'

She jumped as Nick called her name, flushing hotly as she realised that he had stopped beside the tea stall. She had been so lost in thought that she hadn't even noticed. She expected him to pass some comment about her day-dreaming but, surprisingly, he didn't mention it.

'Would you like a cup of tea? Maybe a sandwich. They're always very good and fresh.'

'No, just tea. Thank you. I…I've already got something to eat.'

She heard the strained note in her voice and turned away, afraid of what might be written on her face at that moment. There was a wooden bench close to the stall so she went and sat on it. Thinking about Paul and the way he had betrayed her was so painful even after all this time. Would she ever get over the hurt and humiliation? Or would she forever feel that she could never trust her instincts where men were concerned?

'Here you go. I hope you take milk because I put some in.' Nick placed two plastic cups on the bench between them, then shot her a searching look. 'Are you OK?'

'Fine. Just hungry,' she assured him, although she could hear the hollow ring her voice held even if he couldn't. She busied herself peeling back the lid of the yoghurt carton because she didn't want to check if he *had* heard it. Nick was too astute for her liking, too quick to see through the mask she wore.

They ate in silence for several minutes but Karen was too conscious of him sitting beside her to enjoy her lunch. Each time he picked up his cup, she inwardly flinched in case their arms brushed. When he suddenly crumpled the carton which had held his sandwich and tossed it into the litter bin, she actually jumped.

'Sorry. I seem to have a talent for making you jump,' he observed lightly.

She gave him a quick smile as she got up to throw her empty yoghurt pot in the bin, needing the few seconds it took to get herself in hand. She had to stop acting like this around him all the time. He was just someone she worked with and if she kept that in mind then there wouldn't be a problem.

She went back to the bench, determined to be sensible. 'You said that you wanted to ask my advice. I assume it's about a patient?'

Nick drank the last of his tea, then sighed. 'He soon will be.' He glanced at her and there was a hint of worry darkening his eyes. 'It's my nephew, you see.'

'Jamie?' Karen queried, wondering what he needed her advice for. He was the expert in this field, so surely he knew all the answers?

'I'm not sure that I understand how I can help you,' she admitted uncertainly. 'Is it the operation you're concerned about?'

'Not really. I'm confident that will all go perfectly well, even though it was a battle at first to convince Mel.'

'Your sister-in-law wasn't keen on the idea? But I thought Hugh said she was delighted when he told her it would go ahead?'

Nick must have heard her surprise because he grimaced. 'She is *now*. I think Hugh finally managed to talk her round. However, it's taken some time to convince Mel that any risk to Jamie is negligible compared to the benefits he will derive from having the implant. Ideally, he should have had the operation done a couple of years ago.'

'I imagine it's a worrying time for any parents when they

are faced with the prospect of their child undergoing an operation,' Karen observed softly.

'It is, of course. And for Mel the fear was even greater because of what had happened.' A shadow crossed his handsome face. 'Jamie is all she has left of Ed, you see, and I think she was terrified of something happening to him as well.'

'That's understandable.' Karen chose her words with care because she didn't want him to think that she was prying. However, she couldn't deny that she was curious to learn more about his sister-in-law.

'I take it that Melanie hasn't remarried since the tragedy?'

'No. I keep trying to make her see that her life isn't over but she's so stubborn!' He took a deep breath, making an obvious effort to collect himself. However, Karen had heard the impatience in his voice and put her own interpretation on it.

Was Nick eager to convince Melanie that she still had a future to look forward to because he wanted to be a part of it?

Oddly, her stomach sank at the thought but she had no time to dwell on it because Nick was still speaking.

'Anyway, that isn't the problem. What I wanted from you was some advice about how best to help Jamie once the implant has been done.' He shrugged. 'Obviously, I know all the statistics and understand that it will take time before Jamie's speech improves. But if there is anything we can do to help him...'

He tailed off uncertainly. It seemed so out of character for him to be this hesitant, but Karen guessed that it was because he was involved on a personal level. Nick was obviously devoted to his small nephew.

'Don't push him too hard,' she advised immediately.

'The worst thing you can do to a child with any kind of speech disorder is to put pressure on him. Jamie will have enough to do just adjusting to the changes the implant will make to his life. If he feels that everyone is expecting too much from him then it will make him resentful and that in itself will hinder his progress.'

'That's the last thing I want to do!' Nick sat back against the hard slats of the bench and sighed. 'So you advise time and patience, basically?'

'Yes. You have to remember that the implant isn't a magic cure. Jamie isn't used to hearing normal speech so it will take him time to learn how to reproduce it.' Karen pushed back a wisp of hair as the breeze blew it across her face. She glanced at Nick and was surprised by the expression on his face.

She looked away, shaken by the fact that he should have been looking at her like...well, as a man looked at a woman he was attracted to. She hurried on, anxious to put that idea right out of her head.

'Studies show that it takes more than two years of cochlear implant use before a child can produce intelligible speech and even then it will be limited.'

'So as you said, patience is needed!' He laughed ruefully as he looked at her. There was no hint of anything other than amusement on his face now so Karen found herself relaxing as she realised that she must have imagined what she had seen before.

'Uh-huh. Patience and understanding when he has bad days, as he will. I've dealt with several children who'd had cochlear implants and it was very much a case of taking things slowly. However, they all made such good progress over a period of time that they were able to transfer to mainstream schools eventually,' she added encouragingly.

'That's what we are hoping will happen with Jamie. If

we can just improve his quality of life and ensure that he isn't as isolated from the rest of society we'll be more than happy. Thanks, Karen. I really appreciate your advice and I shall pass it on to Mel.'

He reached over and squeezed her hand. It was all over in a second yet Karen felt her skin tingling from where it had been encased in his strong fingers.

She jumped to her feet, aware that she was trembling. Why she should react like this was beyond her. It had been the briefest touch, no more than a casual gesture of thanks, yet her heart was racing like a steam engine!

'I'd better get back,' she said hurriedly. 'I need to get ready for my afternoon patients.'

'Of course. You must be up to your eyes in it with Denise being off,' Nick agreed as he checked his watch. 'I think I'll play hooky a while longer and get some exercise. Hopefully, a brisk walk round the park should stop me going to seed!'

It had been meant as a joke—however, Karen couldn't stop her eyes from skimming over him. There wasn't an inch of spare fat on him, she thought as she drank in the taut lines of his body.

She turned away with a murmured farewell and hurried back to the hospital so fast that she was out of breath when she got there. She slowed to a more sedate pace and went to her room to prepare for her afternoon patients. It was going to be another busy session from the look of it, but she found it hard to concentrate. Her thoughts kept twisting this way and that yet somehow they always arrived back at one particular subject: Nick Bentley.

It was proving harder than it should have done to get the wretched man out of her head!

CHAPTER FOUR

'WOULD you like to play with some of the toys in that box, Helena? Look, here's a lovely doll; why don't you brush her hair?'

Karen got the child settled then went back to her desk. It was Friday afternoon and the end of her first week in the new job. The days had flown past because she had been so busy. She was looking forward to the weekend so that she could recharge her batteries.

Hopefully, Denise would be back on Monday so things shouldn't be quite so hectic then. However, she had managed to cope in Denise's absence and prove that she was capable of doing the job so it hadn't been too bad a start, not if she discounted the odd way she had acted around Nick Bentley...

She shut off that thought the moment it tried to sneak into her head. She had decided that the only way to deal with the thorny subject of the handsome registrar was by being ruthless. Whenever Nick had appeared in the department, she had made sure that she was too busy to chat. She had also taken to avoiding the canteen *and* the park to avoid running into him. It had meant that breaks were now spent at her desk but she had told herself that was no bad thing in the circumstances. There was certainly plenty of work to be done in Denise's absence so she had concentrated on that.

Now she felt far more confident that the next time she and Nick met there wouldn't be a problem. It had been just a minor hiccup, probably something to do with the fact that he reminded her of Paul in a way. However, it would be most unprofessional to allow her personal feelings to influence her dealings with a colleague so she would be sure to keep them strictly separate in future.

Now Karen took her seat and smiled at Helena's anxious parents. Mr and Mrs Harper-Ward were in their early thirties and three-year-old Helena was their first child. They had been referred by their family doctor as they were worried about Helena's progress and Karen had been asked to do an assessment. She quickly set about reassuring them.

'I really don't think that there is anything to worry about. As you know, the tests have shown that Helena's hearing is excellent. And from what I have seen and heard today her speech and language comprehension is only marginally below average.'

'Really?' Mrs Harper-Ward glanced at her husband, who shook his head. Karen wasn't sure what that was meant to indicate and frowned.

'You appear surprised? Why is that?' she asked cautiously, somewhat at a loss. In her experience, most parents would have been delighted by what she had said. However, that didn't seem to be the case in this instance.

'It's obvious, surely! Oh, I'm sure you only mean to be kind but we would far rather hear the truth and...and try to deal with it!' The woman's voice broke but she made a determined effort to collect herself. She held up her hand when Karen went to speak.

'It hasn't been easy for Jeremy and me to accept there is something wrong but we can't bury our heads in the sand when it's glaringly obvious that there is a problem. Helena should be using *proper* sentences by now, with verbs and everything. Her friends at kindergarten all do so. They can hold a real conversation with you but Helena...well, she just...just *mumbles!* We feel so ashamed!'

'I understand your concerns,' Karen sympathised although her heart had sunk as she'd realised what the problem was. It wasn't the first time that a child had been referred to her because the parents viewed his or her progress as a reflection on themselves. 'However, all children progress at their own pace within certain broad parameters so it's better not to focus too much on comparing your child with her peers as there are bound to be discrepancies.'

'But even the child-care books point to the fact that she is way behind!' Mrs Harper-Ward was becomingly increasing agitated. 'We've kept a record of Helena's progress from the day she was born—how old she was when she first raised her head or tried to crawl, things like that. Everything has been perfect up till now, I assure you. But it's obvious that there is a problem with her speech!'

'That type of chart is a good guideline. However, you must understand that the figures quoted aren't meant to be definitive.' Karen smiled soothingly, hoping to defuse the situation before it deteriorated further. 'In my professional opinion, Helena just needs a little more encouragement, that's all. Nursery rhymes and songs are both marvellous ways of encouraging a child to speak. So is reading aloud to them. Children learn to speak through mimicking the sounds they hear around them so, the more clear speech that Helena hears, the easier it will be for her,' she explained, but it was obvious the Harper-Wards weren't convinced.

'But that's what we do already! Jeremy and I went into this in some depth before Helena was born. We were determined she would have the best start possible so we worked out a timetable which I insist her nanny follows.' Mrs Harper-Ward looked even more distraught as she turned to her husband. 'Tell her, Jeremy!'

'What my wife said is perfectly correct,' he confirmed

pompously. 'Francesca, that's our nanny, knows that once she has collected Helena from kindergarten and given her some lunch, then she must spend the afternoon on *educational* pursuits. We have a chart taped to the fridge detailing exactly what she should be doing at any given point in the day.'

Karen struggled to maintain a neutral expression but she couldn't help thinking that poor little Helena would fare better with a more relaxed approach. 'I understand. But I honestly don't believe that you have any reason to worry. However, I think the best thing would be if I arranged for Helena to come for speech therapy for a few months. Then I shall be able to monitor her progress.'

'Yes, I think so, don't you, Jeremy? Not that we want anyone to find out, of course.' Mrs Harper-Ward shuddered. 'I mean, it isn't the sort of thing you want your friends to know about, is it?'

She shot a horrified look at her child, who was mercifully oblivious as she played with the doll. Karen didn't say anything as she saw the family out. It was wiser not to voice her views although she couldn't help thinking that the Harper-Wards had no idea how lucky they were. When she thought about some of the other cases she had seen that week—children whose speech problems were the result of surgery, for instance—then their concerns seemed out of all proportion.

'Right, that's us finished for the week. Thank heavens!'

Karen looked round with a smile as she heard Josie's exclamation. 'It has been a bit hectic, hasn't it?'

'You can say that again!' The receptionist popped the cover over her computer, then dusted off her hands with a flourish. 'One of the busiest weeks I can remember. I'm glad to see the back of it. Anyway, I think we've earned ourselves a reward for all our hard work, so do you fancy coming for a drink, Karen? A lot of the staff meet up at that wine bar the other side of the park on a Friday night and I'm going over there tonight.'

'Well, I'm not sure...' Karen began then shrugged. 'Why not? The only thing waiting for me at home is a mountain of washing and ironing, and I'm sure it can wait a bit longer!'

'Well, it certainly won't run away,' Josie observed dryly. 'What I need is a nice kind laundry fairy who pops in during the night and does the whole lot for me. With a husband and three teenage boys I seem to spend most of my so-called *free* time up to my neck in dirty jeans and socks!'

Karen laughed. 'And to think I was moaning about the amount I have to do! I think we both deserve a drink, you more than me from the sound of it.'

They left the hospital together and headed across the park. A couple of Josie's friends caught up with them and Karen was introduced all round. By the time they reached the wine bar their numbers had swelled considerably. Josie pointed to a table near the window.

'Grab yourself a seat and I'll get us a drink. It will be like bedlam in here in a few minutes' time.'

Karen went and sat down. She was soon joined by a couple who had followed them into the bar. The woman smiled at Karen as she slid into a seat.

'Hi. I'm Lucy Farrell and this is my husband, Tom. We work at Lizzie's as well, in Neo-natal Intensive Care.'

'Pleased to meet you,' Karen replied, responding immediately to the woman's friendly smile. 'I'm Karen Young, the new speech and language therapist.'

'Oh, we know who you are!' Lucy shot a smiling look at her husband. 'We've heard all about you.'

'Only good things, I hope!' Karen replied with a laugh

although she couldn't help wondering who had been talking about her.

'Could there be anything bad to hear? I'm intrigued, Karen. Come on, what dark secrets are you hiding?'

She felt her heart lurch to a stop as she recognised Nick's deep tones. She swung round, unable to hide her surprise as she found him standing behind her holding three glasses of wine. He set them on the table, then looked quizzically at her.

'Well, come on, then. Confess.'

Lucy laughed. 'Don't be so nosy, Nick! Maybe Karen doesn't want us to know all her darkest secrets.'

'Then I don't know what she's doing working in a hospital!' Tom Farrell grinned as he picked up a glass. 'Most hospitals are hotbeds of gossip and Lizzie's is no exception. It's impossible to keep anything to yourself in that place, believe me!'

Karen joined in the laughter but she had to admit that she was more than a little dismayed by her own stupidity. Why hadn't it crossed her mind that Nick could be at the wine bar? she berated herself.

She forced herself to concentrate as Lucy addressed her again but it wasn't easy to ignore Nick's presence. He had pulled over a stool from a nearby table and placed it next to her chair. The noise level was rising by the minute and when he leaned forward to hear what Lucy was saying Karen couldn't help breathing in the tangy fragrance of his aftershave.

Deliberately, she forced her mind to go blank, refusing to let the delicious aroma stir her senses as it was trying to do. If she didn't let herself think about Nick then she could ignore him. However, it was one thing to come up with the theory and quite another to put it into practice! It was an effort to concentrate on what Lucy was saying with him sitting beside her.

'Sorry, what was that?' she asked. 'I didn't quite catch it.'

'No wonder, with all the racket going on in here!' Lucy grimaced as she raised her voice so that it would carry over the hubbub. 'I was just wondering where you come from, Karen. Although your name has been mentioned, and more than once, I might add, details have been a little thin on the ground.'

Lucy shot a wry look at Nick who smiled innocently back at her. However, Karen was left in little doubt that he was the one who had been talking about her. Her pulse performed that same strange little manoeuvre it had learned to do in the park a few days earlier, a sort of hiccuping somersault, before she determinedly got herself in hand.

So what if Nick *had* mentioned her? What if he was *interested* in her, even? It didn't make a scrap of difference!

'I come from Yorkshire, a small town right in the middle of the Dales,' she replied with as much composure as she could muster.

'Must be a change living here, then,' Tom observed lightly. 'How are you liking it?'

Karen laughed. 'To be honest, I've only been here a week and, as I've been working most of that time, I've not had chance to make up my mind yet!'

'Then you should get someone to show you around and point out all the places of interest.' Lucy turned to Nick. 'You'd be the best qualified, seeing as you were born in London.'

'I'd be delighted. If you want a guided tour then you only have to say the word, Karen, and I'm at your service.'

Nick grinned at her, his eyes full of a warmth she would have needed to be blind not to see. Karen didn't know what to say as it would have been rude to blurt out that he was the last person she would ask to show her around the city. Mercifully, Josie arrived with their drinks at that point and she was spared having to think up a reply as everyone shuffled about making room for her and a couple of her friends to sit down.

Karen found herself wedged against the window with Nick sitting so close beside her that she could feel his thigh pressing against hers each time he moved. She tried to edge away but it was impossible to move more than a few centimetres. The bar had rapidly filled up, mainly with hospital staff, she suspected from the fact that everyone seemed to know one another. There were no free seats left but people were happily propping themselves against walls and squeezing into any gap they could find.

A woman stepped back to let someone get to the bar and cannoned into Nick, who in turn bumped into Karen. He grimaced as he straightened.

'Sorry. This place is a madhouse on Friday nights. Most folk from Lizzie's pop in for a quick one on their way home. It's a way to unwind after the rigours of the week.'

'It is busy,' Karen agreed stiltedly. She took a swallow of her wine, wondering if Josie would be offended if she didn't drink it all. The sooner she left, the better, in her opinion. Although Nick was behaving with the utmost propriety, she was so conscious of him that it was impossible to relax.

She took another large swallow of her drink so that she could hasten her departure, then coughed as some of the wine went down the wrong way. Nick patted her back, his face mirroring concern as he heard her wheezing.

'Hey, are you all right?'

'F-fine...' Karen spluttered a bit more before she finally

managed to catch her breath. 'Some wine went down the wrong way, that's all.'

'You should drink more slowly.' Nick grinned, crooking his little finger as he raised his glass and took an exaggeratedly dainty sip. 'Like this.'

Karen couldn't help laughing. 'I see. Although I think I shall have to practise to get my little finger at just the right angle!'

'You should do that more often, Karen.'

'Do what?' The question popped out before she could stop it. Her smile faded as she stared at him in confusion.

'Laugh. You look like a completely different person when you let yourself relax. I get the feeling that it isn't something you do very often.'

She heard the curiosity in his voice and looked away, uncomfortable with the way he was watching her. Once upon a time she *had* been able to laugh and enjoy life but that had been before she had found out how Paul had used her.

Now she felt foolish tears fill her eyes as she realised that she would have loved to go back to being the person she had been pre-Paul, only it wasn't possible. She couldn't undo the mistakes of the past, just learn a lesson from them.

'I'm sorry. I didn't mean to upset you.' Nick touched her hand and she could hear concern in his voice. 'If there is anything I can do...'

'There isn't. Thank you.'

Karen drew her hand away abruptly and stood up. She knew that Nick was watching her but she didn't look at him. She didn't dare do that when her control was paper thin. It made her feel vulnerable enough to realise that he could see through her so easily.

'Sorry to be a party pooper, folks, but I'd better be off. I've still got tons of things to do with just moving in.' She

fixed a bright smile to her mouth as she turned to Tom and
Lucy Farrell, hoping that they couldn't tell how false it was.
'It was really nice meeting you both.'

'And you,' Lucy replied immediately. 'It's good to see
you in the flesh at last. Although, I have to say that I feel
I already know you!'

Everyone laughed but Karen was hard-pressed to summon a smile. A lot of women would have been flattered by
Nick's interest but she wasn't. She wasn't about to forget
the painful lessons she had learned!

She picked up her bag, murmuring her thanks as Nick
got up to let her pass. There wasn't much room because
they were jammed into the corner so she had to slide past
him.

She felt her breasts brush the hard wall of his chest and
bit back a gasp as her nipples immediately hardened in
response to the contact. Unbidden, her eyes flew to his face
and her heart seemed to stop as she saw the awareness in
his liquid-dark eyes.

She pushed past him, hurrying from the bar as though a
thousand devils were pursuing her. What the others thought
about her abrupt departure she could only guess, just as she
could only guess what Nick thought. He had noticed her
response, that had been obvious. But did he think that it
had meant something, that she was *interested* in him?

Karen bit her lip. She didn't want Nick getting the wrong
idea. She didn't want him getting *any* ideas where she was
concerned! Although she had told herself that she was immune to any man's advances, she was no longer as sure as
she had been.

She took a deep breath, struggling to view what was
happening objectively. Perhaps if she faced up to the situation instead of avoiding it, then she could deal with
it? So...

Fact: Nick Bentley disturbed her.

Fact: he made her feel things she had never expected to feel again.

Fact: she could no longer deny either of the above.

Conclusion: he was strictly off limits from now on.

It was simple really. She just had to make up her mind to avoid him...and stick to it!

She sighed as she made her way to the bus stop. That, of course, was the difficult part of the equation when they had to work together. It seemed she was right back at square one!

CHAPTER FIVE

KAREN spent Friday night catching up on housework. Apart from a week's worth of laundry, she still had unpacking to do. With storage space being at a premium, it was difficult to find room for all her things. However, by the time she finished late that night, the flat looked more like home.

It was amazing what a few pictures and odd bits of china could achieve, she thought, surveying the cosy room. And the other benefit of all her hard work was that she'd had no time to think about Nick Bentley for several hours. Good!

She went to bed, determined to keep up the good work the following day. The bathroom was sorely in a need of a good cleaning and the tiny landing outside her front door badly needed a lick of paint. However, when she awoke shortly before seven on Saturday morning all her good intentions went by the board.

It was a beautiful day and the sliver of sky that she could see from her tiny attic window was the most glorious shade of blue. Bearing in mind that she spent most of her time indoors, it seemed nothing less than a sin not to get out and enjoy the good weather.

That decided, she took a quick shower, turning a blind eye to the spots of mildew which peppered the bathroom walls. It was a beautiful day and she was in the most exciting city in the world. It was about time she saw something of it!

She dressed in her most comfortable jeans and a baggy black T-shirt she had inherited from her younger brother,

Martin, after he'd outgrown it. It had a picture of Bart
Simpson on the front and it always made her smile when
she looked in the mirror. A cosy, cherry-red fleece jacket
completed her outfit.

It was such a relief not to have to dress formally for once
that she made the most of it by tying back her hair with a
black ribbon instead of plaiting it and smoothing on a little
moisturiser instead of bothering with any make-up. So what
if her hair did end up in a riot of curls and her freckles
showed? Did it really matter? It was her day off and she
was going to make the most of it!

Three hours later, after a brief stop for a *café latte* and
a chocolate croissant, Karen found herself in front of
Buckingham Palace. The good weather had brought out the
tourists in droves so there were hundreds of people about.
She caught snippets of conversation in a dozen different
languages as she wended her way through the crowd. When
two elderly American ladies asked if she would take their
photograph, she readily agreed.

Karen handed back the camera amid effusive thanks,
then went on her way. The crowd seemed thicker than ever
so that it was difficult to make any headway. When the
crush of bodies miraculously parted, she stepped smartly
into the gap, then felt her stomach sink as she spotted a
man up ahead. He reminded her so much of Nick Bentley
from the back that she came to an abrupt halt before it
struck her that it couldn't possibly be him.

Nick wouldn't be following the tourist trail when he had
lived in London all his life, nor would he be carrying a
child, piggyback fashion, as this man was doing. However,
there was definitely *something* about the set of those broad
shoulders and glossy black hair which reminded her of
Nick...

Karen groaned as she realised what was happening. Give

her thoughts the proverbial inch and they were soon clock-
ing up the miles!

She swung round, determined to forget about Nick
Bentley for another forty-eight hours. There would be time
enough to think about him when she went into work on
Monday. Hopefully, by then, she would have got things
into perspective. After all, it *had* been an unsettling week
with one thing and another, so it was little wonder that she
had been behaving so strangely.

'Karen? Wait! Hold on there!'

Her footsteps faltered as she recognised an all-too-
familiar voice. She shot a dismayed look over her shoulder
as she realised that it was indeed Nick Bentley. The crowd
suddenly surged forward as the gates to the palace opened
while a car drove out and he disappeared from sight. Karen,
realising this was her chance to escape, promptly took it.

Diving into the crush of people, she made her way as
fast as she could to the other side. She glanced back and
breathed a sigh of relief when she couldn't see anyone following her. With a bit of luck Nick would think that she
hadn't seen him...

She yelped as a heavy hand suddenly descended onto her
shoulder. Even before she'd turned, she knew who it be-
longed to. There was a knowing gleam in Nick's eyes as
he smiled at her which brought a wash of guilty colour to
her cheeks.

'Why do I get the feeling that you were trying to avoid
me?' he asked silkily.

'Don't be silly! Why should I do that?' She rushed on
before he could answer, deeming it wiser. There was no
way that she wanted to go into the ins and outs of why she
had rushed off!

'I didn't realise it was you,' she said quickly, appeasing
her noisy conscience with a half-truth. 'The last thing I'd

have expected you to be doing on a Saturday is sightsee-ing.'

'I promised Jamie that I would bring him to see the Changing of the Guard,' he explained levelly, although she wasn't deaf to the scepticism in his voice. It was obvious that he didn't believe her excuse and once again she found herself wondering how he managed to see through her so easily. It was a relief when he turned his attention to the child at his side.

'This is Karen, Jamie. Say hello to her.' He spoke clearly and slowly, signing the words as he said them. Karen saw the little boy glance uncertainly at her and smiled reassur-ingly at him.

'Hello, Jamie. It's nice to meet you.' She, too, signed as well as said the words, and she saw Nick look at her in surprise.

'Where did you learn to sign?'

'I did a night-school course because I thought it might be helpful,' she explained, glad to steer the conversation towards work. 'A lot of hearing-impaired people use a com-bination of sign language and speech to communicate so I find that it helps, although I don't get to use it all that often.'

'That's brilliant! I'm really impressed, Karen. Not many people would go to so much trouble.'

The scepticism had disappeared now and Karen felt her pulse perform its customary hiccup as she heard the warmth in his voice. She steadfastly ignored it. One—admittedly sincere—compliment wasn't going to make a scrap of dif-ference to her decision to keep him at arm's length.

She looked down as Jamie suddenly tugged on her hand to attract her attention. It was obvious that her ability to speak to him through sign language had dispelled his initial

shyness. His fingers fairly flew as he signed what he wanted
to ask her and Karen laughed.

'Slow down!' She signed the instruction, grinning ruefully at him. 'I'm a bit rusty so you'll have to go really
slowly for me to understand.'

Jamie laughed at that. However, he slowed down as he
repeated his question and this time Karen understood. A
little colour touched her cheeks as she shook her head. 'No,
I just work with your Uncle Nick.'

She looked up as Nick laughed softly. He'd obviously
been following what was happening and there was a light
in his eyes which made Karen's cheeks heat even more.
'So Jamie thinks you're my girlfriend, does he? He has
good taste, I must say.'

She decided to ignore that compliment as well, although
she couldn't help wondering if Nick had really meant it.

She bit back a sigh as she realised what she was doing
once again. Why was it so hard to remain detached where
Nick was concerned? She wasn't vain but she knew that
men found her attractive. Since she'd split up with Paul
several men had asked her out but she'd always refused.
Compliments had left her cold as well. However, there was
something about Nick which made it very difficult to ignore
him. She decided that it was time she went on her way now
that the courtesies had been observed.

She was about to explain that she had to go when once
again Jamie tugged on her hand. Karen frowned as she tried
to follow what he was telling her.

'He's asking if you'd like to come to the zoo with us,'
Nick explained helpfully. 'It's one of his favourite places
to visit when he comes up to London, so I promised to take
him today as a treat.'

'Oh, I don't think so. I mean, it's a lovely idea but I
really couldn't. I…I've loads of things to do back at the

flat with just moving in,' she ad libbed, desperately trying to come up with a plausible excuse. Spend a day with Nick Bentley after the way she had been behaving recently? No way!

Nick relayed her answer to the little boy, shaking his head when Jamie said something else. However, it soon became apparent that the child wasn't happy about her refusal. Karen was dismayed when she saw his lower lip tremble ominously.

'I'm awfully sorry. I didn't mean to upset him.'

Nick sighed as he swung the child into his arms and hugged him. 'It's not your fault, Karen. It's a very unsettling time for him, you have to understand. Mel is trying her best but she's very uptight about the operation and Jamie can sense that something is wrong.

'One of the reasons I offered to bring him out today was to give both of them a break. Mel's staying with my parents so hopefully they will be able to reassure her and she in turn will be able to calm Jamie down. However, I think he's more scared at the thought of going into hospital than anything else.'

'I'm sure he is,' Karen agreed softly, her heart aching as she saw two huge tears forming on the child's thick black lashes. He looked a lot like Nick, she realised, with those huge dark eyes and jet-black brows, although Jamie's hair was fair, not dark like his uncle's.

He was wearing twin hearing aids although she knew that any sound he heard would be extremely limited. She couldn't help thinking how scary it must be for him to be faced with the prospect of communicating with a whole bunch of strangers in the hospital. She would find it daunting and he was just a child. When he suddenly buried his face in Nick's neck and began to cry in earnest, she felt really awful.

The poor child was supposed to be having this day out as a treat and now she had spoiled it for him. Maybe if she agreed to go along just for an hour it would help placate him? After all, there would be loads of other people about so it wasn't as though she and Nick would be on their own.

She came to a swift decision before she could think better of it. 'All right, then, I'll come. But only for an hour, mind. I still have tons of things to do at the flat.'

'Great!' Nick exclaimed. Karen's heart sank as she saw his delighted smile. She couldn't help wondering if he realised that she had agreed to go *purely* for Jamie's sake. However, it was too late to change her mind because Nick had already relayed the news to his nephew.

Karen managed to smile as Jamie clapped his hands with excitement but inside she was quaking as it hit her what she had let herself in for. She had to be mad, quite frankly, stark, staring mad! One whole hour of Nick's company. Sixty minutes of undiluted Bentley charm. Without a doubt, she needed certifying!

'Right, how about something to eat?'

Nick stopped to consult the map, tracing the route they had followed with a well-shaped finger. 'If I'm not mistaken there should be a snack bar along here on the right. Burgers and fries all round, is it?'

'Not for me,' Karen said quickly. The hour had whizzed past as they had looked at the animals. With Jamie there to take the edge off things it had been easier than she'd expected being with Nick. However, she was determined to stick to her original plan.

'I must get back,' she stated firmly. 'I wasn't intending to stay out all day.'

'What a shame. There's still so much left to see.' Nick smiled persuasively. 'Are you sure we can't tempt you to forgo the joys of housework a bit longer? There's a new baby elephant, I believe.'

His right brow crooked. Karen pinned a smile to her mouth, hoping it would belie the fact that her pulse was performing somersaults like a fairground tumbler. Nick looked so handsome standing there, his muscular body clad in slim-fitting jeans and a heavy navy sweater, his black hair slightly mussed by the breeze. Most women would have been only too eager to agree to his pleas, only she wasn't most women. That was the trouble. The legacy of Paul's heartless actions would forever colour her life.

'It's tempting, but I really must get back,' she replied, conscious that Nick was studying her rather too intently for her liking. She turned to Jamie, wondering if Nick had somehow sensed the pain she always felt whenever she thought about Paul. He was so perceptive, so quick to see through her excuses. It made it even more imperative that she kept him at a distance.

She quickly explained to the little boy that she had to go home, shaking her head when Jamie also pleaded with her to stay a bit longer. Nick sighed as he saw his nephew's beseeching expression.

'You seem to have made a real conquest there, Karen. It's unusual for Jamie to take to anyone as quickly as he's taken to you.'

Karen smiled ruefully as the little boy caught hold of her hand and held it tightly. He was obviously loath to let her leave. 'That's probably because I can speak to him. I know how difficult it is for hearing-impaired children to relate to strangers normally.'

'Oh, I think it's more than that.' Nick's voice held a note which made her look curiously at him. 'You have this natural ability to empathise with people, Karen. It's a gift not many people possess.'

'Thank you.' She was deeply touched by what he had said and it was hard not to show it. 'It's very kind of you to say so.'

'It isn't kind, just truthful.' Nick suddenly grinned. 'That being the case, then I'm sure you must realise how desperate Jamie and I are for you to spend more time with us. Come on, Karen, surely you can spare us another hour, *please*?'

'Well...' She hadn't meant to weaken, yet somehow she found herself hesitating.

'I think that's a yes!' Nick exclaimed triumphantly. 'I knew we'd persuade you in the end!'

It was meant as a joke yet Karen couldn't ignore the way her pulse leapt. She took a deep breath to calm her nerves as Nick explained to Jamie what was happening. However, it was hard to get back on even keel. She didn't want to be *persuaded*! She didn't want to be influenced in any way! Yet she knew in her heart that Nick had the power to do both and it scared her.

When he suggested that they had something to eat before they went to see the elephants she raised no objection. It seemed easier to go along with his plans rather than make a fuss. However, she made up her mind that she would excuse herself straight afterwards despite any protests he might make. The sooner he understood that she didn't intend to be coerced into doing things, the happier she would be!

The café was packed with families having their lunch. Nick grimaced as he looked round. 'Every seat seems to be taken. Why don't we buy our lunch and take it outside? There's a picnic area and it won't be so noisy there. It should be just about warm enough to sit outside so long as we find a sheltered spot.'

'Fine by me,' Karen agreed readily. She took hold of

Jamie's hand as they queued up to be served, ordering burger and chips the same as Nick did. Nick was patience itself as Jamie tried to decide what he wanted to eat, showing no sign of irritation as the child changed his mind several times. His attitude was in stark contrast to the man in the next queue to them. He became very agitated when his daughter couldn't decide what she wanted.

Karen sighed as she heard him speak sharply to the little girl before sending her outside with the warning that she would just have to have what she was given. Coming to the zoo was meant to be a treat but she doubted if the little girl would feel it was much fun being spoken to like that.

'Right, that's us sorted.' Nick paid for their food, then carried the tray outside. Several of the picnic benches were taken but he managed to find them a sheltered spot near to some trees.

He set the tray on the table, then treated Karen to a rueful smile. 'I'm sorry there weren't any seats inside. I hope you won't be too cold out here?'

'No, it's fine,' she assured him, sitting down beside Jamie and unzipping her fleece jacket. 'It's hard to believe it's the middle of winter, isn't it? I can't remember the weather being so mild. And I prefer it out here, anyway. It's less noisy and we can enjoy the fresh air while we eat.'

'At least you're not one of those women who wouldn't be seen dead picnicking. They are always too worried about their clothes getting messed up to enjoy eating alfresco,' he observed lightly, bending down to help Jamie pop the tab on his can of cola. Cola suddenly spurted from the can and Karen gasped as most of it showered over her.

'It's a good job, isn't it?' she observed pithily, looking pointedly at her T-shirt while Jamie giggled.

Nick laughed ruefully as he handed her a wad of paper

napkins. 'Sorry. I never intended that to happen. Damn. You've even got cola in your hair. Here, let me mop it up.'

Before Karen could say anything he had crouched down in front of her and started mopping the glistening droplets off her hair. He was so close that she could feel the warmth of his body and smell the fresh scent of his skin.

A frisson rippled under her skin, a combination of heat and awareness which made her breath catch. Nick must have heard the slight sound she made because he immediately stopped what he was doing.

'Sorry. Did I snag a hair?'

'I...it doesn't matter.' She heard the husky note in her voice and hurriedly averted her face. Crumpling up the napkins, she dabbed at the stains on her T-shirt as Nick moved away. It was difficult to behave naturally but the fear that he might guess what had caused her to react like that was the best inducement in the world.

She tossed the soiled napkins onto the tray with what she hoped was a nonchalant smile. 'That will have to do. It's only an old T-shirt of my brother's, anyway.'

'Ah, I did wonder.' Nick had sat down and opened the carton containing his burger. He bit off a mouthful and chewed it before continuing. 'I didn't have you down as a Bart Simpson fan, to be honest. It doesn't gel with your image.'

'What image?' Karen asked in surprise.

'Oh, you know—the cool, calm, dedicated professional.' His grin was teasing but that didn't mean she couldn't see the curiosity in his eyes. 'Maybe that's just a front and this is the *real* you. It makes me wonder if I should be asking, Will the real Karen Young stand up, please?'

'You'd be disappointed if you did. What you see is what you get, I'm afraid!' She managed to laugh but the question had unsettled her, hinting once again at how astute he was. 'Sorry!'

'Oh, don't apologise because I happen to have an over-active imagination. Anyway, ignore my ramblings. Tell me about your brother. Is he older or younger than you and what is his name?'

'His name is Martin and he's eighteen, six years younger than me,' Karen replied, relieved to change the subject. She didn't want Nick speculating about her, didn't want to arouse his interest in any way. It was safer to let him think that the bland professional image she took such care to project was the real her.

Maybe it was. When she thought about the warm, loving, *trusting* woman she had been once upon a time she had difficulty recognising herself as that person. Paul had changed her; he had destroyed her ability to trust anyone ever again.

'And what does your brother do? Is he still at school?'

She shook her head, glad to have something to focus on rather than such unhappy thoughts. 'No, he's about to start university. He's going to read law at Liverpool, although I think studying will be a sideline to his social life!'

Nick laughed. 'Well, he's in the right place for it! I went to med school in Liverpool and loved it. There is always something to do there and the people are great.'

'Praise indeed coming from a southerner!' Karen laughed, feeling able to relax now that the conversation was on safer ground. 'You don't adhere to the Watford Gap theory, then, I take it?'

'That there is no life north of there?' He immediately understood what she'd meant and laughed deeply. 'Certainly not! I love the north of England and would have happily stayed there if it weren't for the fact that I always wanted to work at Lizzie's. But what about you? What made you decide to relocate?'

Karen shrugged. 'I always wanted to work with children,' she said shortly.

'I see. But it must have been a wrench leaving your friends and family?' he probed softly.

'I wanted a...' she had been going to say that she'd wanted a fresh start but she knew that would be too revealing so quickly amended it '...a new challenge. Working at Lizzie's was exactly what I'd been looking for.'

'So there's no one back home pining for you?' he asked lightly, yet she could hear the curiosity in his voice.

She looked him squarely in the eyes, wanting there to be no mistake about what she was saying. 'No, there's nobody. The only thing I'm interested in at the moment is my career and making a success of it.'

Nick shrugged. 'You might think that now, but it isn't always possible to choose when you fall in love. Sometimes it can just happen and there isn't a thing you can do about it.'

'Not in my case!' she stated, then wished she hadn't sounded quite so adamant when it might arouse his suspicions. It was a relief when Jamie suddenly interrupted them by asking if he could play on the swings.

Nick went with him while Karen set about clearing away the remains of their lunch. However, as she took the rubbish to the litter bin she couldn't help feeling a trifle despondent. She had always dreamed of a home and family, a man to love and love her in return, but it would never happen now. Oh, she had her work and she enjoyed it, but was it really enough? Yet the thought of ever allowing herself to fall in love again scared her. How could she risk that ever happening again when she had been hurt so badly?

'Leanne...Leanne! Oh, help me, someone, *please*!'

Karen looked round as she heard the scream, although at first she couldn't see where it was coming from. However, people were hurrying towards the picnic tables so she assumed it must have come from there.

'What's going on?' Nick demanded, coming back to find out what all the commotion was about.

'I don't know.' Karen craned her neck to see what was happening and just then the crowd parted. She could just make out a figure lying on the ground close to one of the tables. 'It looks like someone is hurt…a child, I think.'

'I'd better go over there and see if I can help,' Nick said quickly.

'I'll look after Jamie,' she told him, taking hold of the boy's hand as Nick hurried away.

She and Jamie followed him to where the crowd had gathered. Nick had pushed his way through the onlookers and was already kneeling beside the little girl by the time Karen got there. It was the child Karen had noticed in the café earlier and her heart sank as she saw how ill she looked. It was obvious even to her untrained eyes that the little girl was having difficulty breathing, although she had no idea what the problem was.

'Can someone ring for an ambulance?' Nick demanded, looking up. He spotted Karen and beckoned her over as a man produced a mobile phone and called the emergency services. She pushed her way through the crowd and sat Jamie on the bench before hurrying to Nick's side.

'Can you give me a hand here, Karen?' he asked as she knelt beside him. 'I need you to find something to put under her legs to raise them. She's having trouble breathing and I need to increase the blood supply to her heart and brain.'

Karen looked round and quickly spotted a large shopping bag beside the table. She ran to fetch it and propped the child's legs up on it but her breathing didn't improve.

'She looks dreadful, Nick,' she said in concern as she watched the little girl gasping for air. 'Do you know what happened?'

'I can guess,' he replied grimly, gently positioning the child's head so that he could begin CPR if it was needed. 'It looks very much like a severe allergic reaction to something or other. The symptoms are classic signs of anaphylactic shock.'

Karen frowned. 'You mean like a reaction to a wasp or a bee sting?'

'Yes, but that's unlikely at this time of year. It's probably something she's eaten.' He looked up, his gaze going straight to the child's distraught mother. 'Is your daughter allergic to anything?'

'Yes, nuts. But she hasn't had any. We're always so careful...!' Her voice turned into a wail but Nick's tone was firm.

'I know how upset you are but you must try to help me. Has she had an attack like this before?'

'Just once. But it wasn't as bad as this,' the mother replied, making an effort to collect herself.

'Did you take her to a doctor? And did he give you anything to carry with you in case it ever happened again?' he persisted.

Karen was impressed by his composure as he prised information out of the distressed woman. Despite how urgent the situation was, he remained totally in control, never once betraying any hint of panic.

'Yes!' The woman looked frantically around. 'They gave me something to inject Leanne with but my husband's got it in his pocket and I don't know where he is!'

She began to sob loudly as Nick turned to the man who had phoned for the ambulance and rattled out instructions.

'Get back onto the ambulance control centre and tell

them that I'm almost certain it's an allergic reaction to nuts and that we need adrenaline and antihistamines here stat!'

The man hurriedly put through a second call. However, before he could finish it Nick swore softly. 'Damn! She's arrested. Quick, Karen, do exactly as I tell you to. I need you to breathe into her mouth while I massage her heart. One breath to every five compressions but take it gently because she's only a child. Got that?'

Karen nodded although her own heart felt as though it were about to seize up as she realised the enormity of what was happening. She was trembling as she watched Nick palpate the child's chest. He glanced at her and there was such confidence in his gaze that it immediately steadied her. If Nick thought she could do it, then so she could!

She breathed gently into the child's mouth and was overcome with relief when she saw the little chest rise.

'Good. That's perfect.'

Nick's words of encouragement helped enormously. Her confidence was bolstered by his belief in her. She counted as he performed another series of chest compressions then did her bit, sending another breath of life-giving air into the child's limp body.

Silence fell as the crowd watched what was happening. Even the girl's mother had stopped sobbing and was standing, pale and trembling, as she watched what was going on. Karen lost count of the number of times they repeated the procedure before she heard the welcome wail of an ambulance's siren. When the paramedics arrived she was more than happy to relinquish her place at the little girl's side.

Nick stayed with them, helping as the child was intubated and given injections of adrenaline and antihistamines. They were just about to load the stretcher into the back of the ambulance when the girl's father appeared.

'What's going on?' he demanded, pushing his way through the crowd.

'It's Leanne. She had one of those attacks…couldn't breathe and everything and you'd gone off with that pen thing in your pocket. I don't know how it happened because we're always so careful…'

The girl's mother suddenly stopped and stared at him in horror. 'You did check the wrapper on that ice cream before you gave it to her, didn't you, Dave?'

The father turned pale. 'Well, no. I mean, it was only an ice cream…'

He trailed off and Nick sighed. 'I don't suppose you've still got the wrapper, have you?'

'It should be in this bag of rubbish.' The girl's mother hunted it out and handed it to him. Nick skimmed through the list of ingredients and nodded.

'Yes, there's the culprit: ground nut oil. There was probably only a trace of it in the product but you don't need very much to trigger an allergic reaction.'

'You stupid thing! Fancy giving her that! I can't believe that you'd be so…so careless!'

The little girl's mother was still berating her husband as they climbed into the ambulance. It drove away with sirens blaring. Karen shook her head in dismay.

'It's incredible how easily something like that can happen, isn't it? I mean, who'd imagine there'd be any danger in giving a child an ice cream?'

'It is scary. Some children are so sensitive to nuts that even the *smell* of them can send them into shock,' Nick agreed soberly.

'Do you think she will be all right, though?' Karen asked worriedly.

'Oh, I think so. Those injections she had usually work like magic. She should be right as rain in a day or so, and it's thanks to you, Karen. You were brilliant just now. You responded like a real pro, in fact!'

'I was just the sidekick. You did all the hard work,' Karen replied with a smile, although she was beginning to feel a bit shaky now that reaction was setting in.

'I'd say it was a team effort, then. It just shows what can be achieved when people work together,' he replied lightly before he suddenly caught sight of her white face. 'Hey, are you OK?'

'Just a bit wobbly,' she admitted tremulously. 'Must be reaction. I'm not used to being involved in a life-or-death situation. I don't know how you doctors do it, quite frankly.'

Nick shrugged. 'We're trained to respond in an emergency so it's a bit easier for us, although it still has an effect.'

'Does it?' She looked at him and saw immediately that he was telling the truth. Funnily enough, it didn't surprise her now that she thought about it. As she had watched Nick struggling to save the child's life it had been obvious how much he had cared, so it was bound to have affected him.

Karen took a deep breath as the thought settled into her mind. She wasn't sure why it bothered her, yet it did. Why should it matter that Nick couldn't maintain a professional detachment towards his work? She had no idea, but it felt as though the discovery had changed things and that she could no longer view him in quite the same light as she had before.

It was a relief when Jamie came over to them just then because it meant that she didn't have to think about it any more. Maybe it was silly, but even acknowledging that there were things about Nick she admired seemed like a mistake.

They spent the next few minutes answering Jamie's

questions and reassuring him that the little girl was going to be all right. Nick sighed in relief as Jamie went racing back to the swings.

'At least that seems to have settled his mind. I didn't want him getting upset about what he had seen.'

'I think he should be OK now,' Karen agreed. 'He seems a happy, well-balanced child.'

'He is. Mel has done a brilliant job of bringing him up. It can't have been easy on her own. Still, with a bit of luck, all that will change soon.'

Karen wasn't sure what he'd meant by that. Was Melanie thinking of getting married again? But who to?

Her heart lurched as it struck her that Nick might be the prospective bridegroom. It made sense because it was obvious how fond he was of his sister-in-law and how devoted he was to Jamie. However, it didn't explain why the thought should worry her.

She sighed, realising that she was getting too involved in this situation. Frankly, it was way past time that she brought the afternoon to a close. When Nick started to follow Jamie towards the playground she hung back.

'I think I'd better be on my way home now,' she explained when he looked round to see where she was. 'It's been great but I've loads to do back at the flat.'

'Of course. We mustn't take up any more of your day,' he said evenly. 'I'm grateful that you spared us so much of your time, Karen. I know Jamie enjoyed having you with us.'

Meaning that he hadn't?

Karen closed her mind to the insidious little voice which had whispered that in her ear. It made no difference to her if Nick had been glad of her company purely for the sake of his nephew, she assured herself as he sketched her a wave and walked away. In fact, she was pleased! It meant that she'd been wrong to assume that he was interested in her when all he had been trying to do was to be friendly.

She should have been reassured to realise that, but she wasn't. She felt decidedly piqued, if the truth be told. She sighed as she made her way to the exit. It seemed that she couldn't win where Nick was concerned!

CHAPTER SIX

'I'M SORRY you got dropped in at the deep end like that, Karen. Although from what I've heard, you coped marvellously!'

It was Monday morning and Karen had arrived at work to find that Denise was back. She had spent the rest of the weekend working in her flat despite the fact that the good weather had continued. However, she had refused to be tempted to play truant a second time. Frankly, she preferred to forget what had happened on Saturday. It had been a mistake to go with Nick because it had left her feeling more mixed up than ever.

She *wasn't* interested in him so why did the thought of his relationship with his sister-in-law bother her so much?

Karen sighed as once again the answer eluded her. However, now wasn't the time to be worrying about it. She focused her attention on what Denise was saying as the older woman brought two cups of coffee to the desk.

'Ever had the feeling that we've been here before?' Denise asked ruefully. 'It seems longer than a week since we sat here drinking coffee, doesn't it?'

'It certainly does. How is your son, anyway? I was surprised you were here today; does that mean he's improving?'

'Thankfully, yes. Peter is such a lot better that he's being transferred to a hospital closer to home tomorrow. My husband has stayed on in Oxford so he can be near him but I decided to come back.' Denise smiled. 'I didn't want you thinking that I'd abandoned you completely!'

Karen laughed. 'You shouldn't have worried. Josie and I coped...just! Fortunately, she managed to cancel most of your list apart from the odd few she couldn't get in touch with. Most people were very understanding with one notable exception.' She sighed. 'Kevin Walters' father kicked up a fuss when he found out you weren't here so I decided to see Kevin myself. I hope that was all right but I felt so sorry for the child.'

'Of course it was all right. And I know exactly what you mean. Tony Walters is a horrible man, isn't he? Many a time I've had to bite my tongue to stop myself saying something when I've heard him bullying that poor boy!' Denise declared heatedly.

'It's an awful way to treat a child, isn't it? I couldn't believe that any parent could be so cruel,' Karen concurred.

'That's the trouble, though. He *isn't* Kevin's real father.'

'No?' Karen couldn't hide her surprise and she heard Denise sigh.

'No. I managed to get the whole story out of his mother a few months ago when she brought Kevin in for his appointment. She told me that she'd had an affair while her husband was working abroad and that Kevin was the result of it.' Denise shrugged. 'Evidently, they agreed to forget about it and try to make their marriage work but obviously Tony Walters still bears a grudge.'

'Which he's taking out on Kevin. The poor boy! His life must be purgatory.' Karen frowned. 'Mr Walters said something about him only bringing Kevin here because he had to...something about the courts, if I'm not mistaken?'

'You're not. Kevin was first assessed as needing therapy when he was five, as you probably gathered from his notes. However, his parents never kept the appointments.' Denise shook her head sadly. 'The family moved house and changed education authorities so somehow Kevin slipped through the net. It was only when he started at his present school that his head teacher became concerned about the problems Kevin was having and contacted the social services department. The upshot of it all was that his social worker applied for a supervision order, stating that Kevin must be brought for speech therapy. However, his attendance has been patchy so we're having to monitor the situation.'

'I understand now. No wonder the poor boy was so withdrawn at first. I had the devil of a job getting any kind of response from him,' Karen explained, realising sadly that the situation was worse than she'd imagined it to be.

'You mean Kevin actually *said* something to you?' Denise sounded incredulous as she put her cup down and stared at Karen.

'Why, yes. Just by chance I happened to have this book on wildlife with me and it seemed to spark Kevin's interest. Evidently, he's passionate about birds.' She frowned. 'I take it that you've not had any luck with him, then?'

'I certainly haven't! In fact, I'd asked one of the psychologists for help to see if he could suggest anything. However, Kevin refused to co-operate when I arranged for him to be seen so I got nowhere. Well done, you! That was a real breakthrough.'

Karen blushed with pleasure although she modestly shook her head. 'I'm sure it was just a fluke. I mean, if I hadn't happened to have that book—'

She broke off as someone knocked on the door and Denise called out to tell them to come in. She felt heat suffuse her as Nick appeared. She looked down at her notepad as he came over to the desk, trying to quell the noisy thundering of her heart. However, she was so conscious of him standing beside her that it was impossible to control it. Her only consolation was that Nick couldn't possibly have guessed the effect he'd had on her.

'I just saw Josie and she told me you were back,' he said warmly to Denise. 'How's your son doing?'

'He's much better, thank you.' Denise quickly brought him up to date on her son's progress, then laughed ruefully. 'Mind you, I don't think I needed to worry about what was going on here in my absence. Karen seems to have coped very well without me!'

Nick gave Karen a warm smile. 'She's a real trooper! She's fitted in just fine. I couldn't imagine what the place would be like without her now.'

He turned back to Denise, mercifully missing the tide of colour which swept up Karen's cheeks. Had Nick meant that? she wondered dizzily before she managed to get herself in hand.

She stood up, fixing a smile to her mouth as the other two stopped talking and looked at her. 'I'd better get started. I'm due to visit a child on the oncology unit and I don't want to be late and get in the way of any ward rounds.'

'I'll come with you,' Nick said at once. 'I was on my way upstairs when I bumped into Josie.' He started to leave, then glanced back at Denise.

'Before I forget, Mel is bringing Jamie in today. His implant is going ahead and Hugh has him scheduled for first thing tomorrow morning.'

'That's brilliant news, Nick!' Denise declared warmly. 'You must be so pleased because you've waited long enough to get it all sorted out.'

'I'm thrilled. And so is Mel, believe it or not.' He laughed deeply as he shook his head. 'The power of love, eh? It works all sorts of miracles!'

Denise laughed but Karen wasn't sure what Nick had

meant by that odd statement. Had he been talking about Melanie's love for her son or what?

It was impossible to tell unless she asked him for an explanation and that was the last thing she felt like doing. What if Nick told her that the reason his sister-in-law had accepted the idea of Jamie having the operation was because *he* had persuaded her? Karen knew how persuasive Nick could be, so how much more difficult would it be for a woman to refuse his pleas if they shared a loving relationship?

'Is it your first visit to Oncology?'

Karen blinked as she realised that they had arrived at the lifts without her being aware of it. She forced the disquieting thoughts to the back of her mind, deeming it both safer and wiser to concentrate on work rather than on matters which had nothing to do with her. However, she couldn't deny the ache which filled a small corner of her heart as she looked at him and thought about his relationship with Melanie. How odd that it should feel as though she had suffered some sort of a loss when she'd had nothing to lose in the first place.

'Erm, yes, it is. So far I've seen all my patients in my office but apparently this child isn't well enough to leave the ward.' She glanced at her notes, glad of the excuse to focus on something other than his handsome face. 'I have to see someone called Graham Woods. Is that right?'

'That's it. Gray's specialist reg on the oncology unit. A great bloke, too. You'll like him.'

The lift arrived and Nick stepped aside for her to precede him, then pressed the buttons for their floors. The doors closed and he leant against the steel-clad wall as he looked quizzically at her.

'No after-effects from Saturday's drama, I hope?'

Karen managed to laugh although her voice sounded a

little more strained than she would have liked. 'None at all, although I must say that I wouldn't want to go through that again! It was quite scary knowing that it was down to us whether or not that little girl made it.'

'It was but you were brilliant, Karen. I couldn't have asked for a better team-mate. I was telling my parents about what you did and they were very impressed, especially my father.'

Nick grinned as he saw her brows rise. 'Dad was head of trauma care at St Luke's until he retired last year. Now he lectures on the subject all round the world.'

'I only did what anyone else would have done,' she said quickly. 'And I'm sure my contribution was a very minor part of the whole operation.'

'Not at all. If I'd had to perform CPR by myself then it would have been far more difficult. If you don't believe me, then ask the expert.'

The lift came to a halt as it reached his floor and the doors opened. He put out his hand to stop them closing as he paused. 'Mum's throwing a surprise birthday party for my father a week on Saturday. How about coming along? I know he'd love to meet you in the flesh at last.'

Karen wasn't sure what he'd meant by that. Nick had made it sound as though she had been the topic of conversation at his parents' home for some time but that couldn't be right.

She didn't dwell on it, however, as she had a far more pressing problem to contend with, namely thinking up an excuse. The last thing she wanted was to accept his invitation after how mixed up she'd felt since Saturday!

'It's very kind of you,' she began.

'But you're washing your hair?' Nick laughed but there was a gleam in his eyes which sent a wave of heat racing through her veins.

'No,' she snapped, then took a deep breath, aware that it was unwise to rise to his baiting. 'I'm not washing my hair but I do have things to do, I'm afraid.'

'And you can't manage to find a window in your busy schedule and spare an hour to have some fun?' His mouth pursed as he looked at her. Karen shifted uncomfortably as his gaze travelled from the top of her immaculate head to the tips of her equally immaculate shoes before he sighed.

'I think I like the out-of-hours Karen better. The one who doesn't mind getting showered in cola and picnicking outside in the middle of winter. Once you put on that smart suit and fasten back your hair you turn into a different person.'

Karen's breath caught as he reached out and caught hold of her chin to tilt her face towards the light. 'You've even blotted out those adorable freckles, I see. Why, Karen? That's what I can't help wondering. Why go to so much trouble to hide the warm, caring woman I just know that you are behind that frosty exterior?'

His thumb brushed across her mouth in the lightest of caresses which could have been construed as accidental if it weren't for the look in his eyes. Karen felt a lump come to her throat as she saw the concern in the look he gave her. She had a sudden urge to pour out the whole miserable story, to tell him who and what had made her into the person she was.

The words were actually hovering on her lips when his pager beeped. Nick held her for a second longer, then abruptly let her go and stepped out of the lift. The doors slid shut and Karen leant against the cold steel wall as the lift whisked her upwards. She could feel herself trembling but she couldn't control the spasms which ran through her body just as she couldn't erase Nick's words from her mind.

How she longed to be as he had described her: warm and caring! But she was afraid to let down her defences, afraid of making a mistake, afraid of having her heart broken as it hadn't really been broken before...

The lift came to a halt but she didn't move. Her head was whirling as she tried to get to grips with that thought. If Paul hadn't broken her heart, then what had he done? Was it really only anger at the way she had been used which made her feel this way?

It was too much to take in let alone rationalise at that moment. But as she went to step from the lift she caught a glimpse of herself reflected in the metal wall. The image was hazy and distorted, like a reflection in a funhouse mirror at a fairground. It didn't look like her, she realised with a sense of shock, didn't look like the person she *knew* she was. It was a pale imitation, drained of life and colour, leeched of everything which was essentially *her*. This was the legacy Paul had bequeathed her, this colourless, timid woman who hid from the world rather than face it.

It was a shock and a revelation. Somehow, what had made sense before made little now. If she wanted to leave the past behind then she had to face the future head on. She couldn't do that by denying who and what she was or it would be a lie. All she needed was the courage to take that first step.

'Good, Ian. Well done.'

Karen leant over and gently hugged the boy, taking care not to snag the IV line which was feeding him a potent cocktail of drugs. Ian Banks was thirteen years old and suffering from a massive brain tumour. It was hoped that the drugs would shrink the tumour enough so that it could be surgically removed.

Gray Woods, the SR, had explained it all to her before

Karen had been introduced to the child. His face had been grim as he had added that Ian had less then a twenty-per-cent chance of coming through the operation but that keeping his spirits up was vital. That was why she had been asked to see the boy.

The tumour had left Ian with Broca's asphasia, a language disorder resulting from damage to the front portion of the language-dominant side of his brain. Ian spoke in short, clipped sentences, often omitting small words such as 'and' or 'the'. However, he understood whatever was said to him and was very aware and upset by what was happening.

Normally, Karen would have waited until after the operation to suggest therapy but in this case she had decided that it would help keep Ian's spirits up to provide any help she could.

Now she sat back and gave the boy a warm smile. 'I don't want to tire you out. Shall we stop now?'

She was careful to speak slowly and use short sentences which would help his comprehension and, obviously, Ian had followed every word because he shook his head.

'Stay…longer…' He reached for a magazine on his bed-side locker. 'Show…this.'

Karen took it from him, smiling as she saw that it was a magazine published by the Royal Society for the Protection of Birds. 'How lovely. Are you a bird-watcher?'

Ian nodded. Most of his hair had fallen out as a result of the chemicals his body was being bombarded with and it gave him the appearance of an old man but with a child's face and body.

'Like birds…lot. Dad takes…' He tailed off uncertainly.

'Your dad takes you bird-watching. How lovely.' Karen didn't miss a beat as she kept the conversation flowing. Ian's speech problems meant that he'd become very isolated as it was difficult for him to keep up a conversation with the other children in the ward. Although his friends and family came in regularly to visit him and the staff did as much as they could, Karen suspected that he felt very lonely at times.

She flicked through the magazine while he pointed out different birds, knowing how therapeutic it would be for him to talk to someone about his hobby. However, it was when she came to an article on kestrels that a thought occurred to her.

What if she introduced Ian to Kevin Walters? The two boys shared a common interest and both were badly in need of a friend. It seemed like such a good idea but she decided that it would be better not to mention it to Ian until she had talked it over with his doctors.

'Going soon. When…leave here,' Ian told her hesitantly as they reached the last page.

Karen's heart ached as she put the magazine back on his locker. She couldn't help wondering if Ian would ever be well enough to go bird-watching again. Certainly his prognosis wasn't all that great. However, she didn't betray her concerns as she said goodbye and promised to go back and see him the following day.

She left the ward, stopping at the office on her way out to see if Gray Woods was still around. He wasn't there but there was a very pleasant young woman doctor by the name of Lucy Brett, who listened carefully to Karen's suggestion that Ian might benefit from speaking to another boy who was interested in the same things as he was.

Lucy agreed to check with Gray and get back to her so Karen went on her way. It was almost time for her break so on a sudden whim she decided to go to the canteen. She couldn't keep hiding away in her office in case she ran into Nick. It was ridiculous, quite frankly. Anyway, he would probably be tied up with his sister-in-law if she was coming in that morning…

She cut that thought dead, refusing to afford it any leeway as she made her way to the canteen. Josie was there so Karen bought herself a cup of coffee and a scone, then went to join her.

'Oh, the joys of not having to watch your weight!' Josie declared, enviously watching Karen spread butter and jam on her scone. 'Some people just make you sick, don't they?'

She glanced over Karen's shoulder, obviously including someone else in the conversation. 'Look at her, slim as a wand and beautiful to boot. It isn't fair!'

'I know what you mean, Josie. So much all wrapped up in one beautiful package.'

Karen's head flew round as she recognised Nick's voice. He treated her to a teasing smile but she couldn't help but see the appreciative gleam in his eyes. 'I wonder if the board knew what they were doing by hiring Karen. I bet I'm not the only guy around here smitten by her charms!'

Josie laughed, taking what he'd said as a joke. Maybe he'd meant it as that but Karen couldn't help wondering…

She picked up her cup of coffee and took a swallow of the hot liquid, refusing to think about what Nick had or hadn't meant!

'As I said, some folk have all the luck. Anyway, what have you got there, Nick?' Josie asked cheerfully. 'A pressie by the look of it, but who for?'

'Oh, it's just a little something for Karen.' He dropped a gaily wrapped parcel on the table beside her. 'It's to make up for what happened at the zoo. I happened to spot it on my way into work this morning and couldn't resist buying it. It's just so *you*.'

Karen didn't know what to say. She stared at the parcel

in much the way she might have viewed a particularly dangerous animal…warily and with dismay.

'For me?' she muttered, her voice thick with a mixture of embarrassment and apprehension. The first was because she could see heads turning their way as people craned their necks to see what was happening and the second because she had no idea what the parcel might contain!

'Well, aren't you going to open it, then?' Josie demanded, obviously dying of curiosity to see what it contained. She suddenly laughed and gave Karen a knowing wink. 'Or perhaps it's something which would be best opened in private?'

'I…erm…of course not!' Karen snapped, jolted out of her inertia by the thought of what people might be thinking. She quickly ripped open the brightly coloured paper, then stared dazedly at what it had contained.

'It will make up for the one that got ruined the other day. And I thought it was very appropriate…in so many ways.'

Nick's tone was silky as he picked up the T-shirt. He shook it out with a flourish and held it against his own chest so that Karen could see the picture printed on its front.

She swallowed but it was difficult to know what to say. Everyone else just laughed as they saw the picture of the fairy-story heroine, Rapunzel, printed on the T-shirt. True to the old tale, she was perched in her castle turret with the prince standing below and beseeching her to let him climb up to her.

Karen knew that everyone had assumed that Nick had chosen the T-shirt because Rapunzel had long hair like she had. But was that his *only* reason or did Nick see her as that princess, locked away in her own kind of tower? And was he, like the prince in the fairy tale, asking to be let into her life? Or was she reading too much into what had been meant purely as a bit of fun?

It was a relief when Josie chipped in, taking the T-shirt off Nick and holding it against Karen while she gave it her due consideration. 'I'd say it was a perfect likeness! Come on, Karen, confess. When you're not working here you double as a model for T-shirt artists!'

Everyone laughed at that, Karen included because it was such a relief to have been let off the hook. 'How did you guess?'

She took the shirt off Josie and folded it neatly, then placed it on the table beside her plate. Nick hadn't said anything to either deny or confirm what Josie had said and Karen didn't intend to give him the opportunity. Some questions were best left unanswered!

'Thank you,' she said formally. 'Although, you really shouldn't have bothered. The cola stains washed out of my old T-shirt.'

'I'm glad to hear it. Anyway, I'm glad you like this one. I hoped you would...appreciate it.'

There was a nuance in his voice which answered the question she hadn't wanted answering. Karen's face must have betrayed her because his eyes gentled as they held hers.

'The best thing about fairy stories is that they always have happy endings.'

Tears prickled her eyes and she looked down at her plate as he walked away. Nick obviously had guessed that there was something in her past which had hurt her and wanted to reassure her that she, too, would find the happy ending. She was touched by his concern but it was a relief that Josie apparently didn't notice anything amiss.

She had grown too used to keeping her feelings to herself to find it easy to open up and thankfully she didn't have to. Josie happily chattered away for the rest of their break-time; she was obviously amused by the gift and curious to know what had prompted it.

Karen explained what had happened because it seemed wiser not to make too much of a mystery out of her meeting with Nick and subsequent visit to the zoo. She certainly didn't want Josie thinking that it had been a date or anything like that! However, despite sticking rigidly to the facts, she sensed that Josie's imagination was running away with her.

She sighed as they went back to their department where the receptionist lost no time in knocking on Denise's door on the pretext of asking her something or other. Karen knew it was just a ruse and that Josie was probably regaling Denise with the story.

So what would happen next? Would they add up the requisite two and two then come up with the usual wrong answer? Karen thought wryly. Probably! After all, she wasn't Rapunzel and Nick wasn't a prince. Although she was touched by his gesture, it made no difference. If she wanted to stay in her tower, then she would jolly well do so!

Well, probably. Maybe? Perhaps?

CHAPTER SEVEN

ANOTHER week passed and Karen felt more firmly established in her new job. There were always small variations about the way things were done in any profession but she soon slipped into the Lizzie's way of thinking.

The children came *first* and nothing was too much trouble for the staff if it was for the benefit of their patients.

It was a view which Karen found both heartening and demanding because it meant that she was expected to give one hundred and *ten* per cent in everything she did. She rose to the challenge and by the start of her third week knew that she'd made the right decision about moving to London. If only her personal life didn't feel as though it were at rock-bottom then life would have been perfect, but she couldn't have everything.

Nick continued to be a frequent visitor to the department so she saw him most days and he never failed to disturb her. It didn't matter if she just happened to see him walking across Reception or waiting for the lift, he *always* left her feeling unsettled although she refused to work out why.

Karen knew that his nephew had had his operation and that it had gone well. She had gleaned that from Hugh when she'd happened to share the lift with him the day after the operation had taken place. Hugh had seemed to take it for granted that Karen would be anxious for news so he had told her all about it.

Karen suspected that people had put their own interpretation on the T-shirt episode and that Josie had contributed in no small way to the assumption that she and Nick were an 'item'. It bothered her that everyone had got the wrong idea but there wasn't a lot she could do about it. She contented herself with the thought that the rumours would die down in their own good time. When Nick went off to attend a conference in Edinburgh, it seemed like a blessing. The only trouble was that Karen discovered that she missed seeing him about. Crazy!

She got into work on the Friday to find Denise scurrying about. Although most of their work was done on a one-to-one basis, there were group sessions for the children as well and that morning they were expecting half a dozen under-fives.

'You look harassed,' Karen observed lightly as she shed her coat and went to help. 'What do you want me to do first?'

'If you can get the spare toys out of the cupboard—' Denise began, then stopped dead. 'Good heavens, don't you look different!'

Karen shrugged self-consciously as she saw the surprise on the older woman's face. 'You warned me to dress casually,' she explained, wondering if she'd been right to opt for jeans and a T-shirt. The fact that it was the shirt Nick had bought for her had given her a few misgivings but it had been the most colourful one she'd been able to find. Most of her wardrobe was rather drab—plain blouses and sensible T-shirts in neutral colours—and this had seemed far more appropriate for what they had planned, although she certainly wouldn't have worn it if Nick had been around.

'Oh, I wasn't meaning that you shouldn't have worn that outfit!' Denise said hurriedly. 'It's great and just right for a morning where we shall no doubt end up scrabbling around the floor. It's just that you look...well, so much more *relaxed* than you usually do.'

'Do I?' Karen shot a surprised look at her clothes again.

'Yes, and I do think that is important in this job.' Denise took a deep breath but it was obvious that she had been wanting to say something for some time. 'You always look great, Karen, but I have been meaning to suggest that you opt for a more casual look. I just wasn't sure how to go about it, to be honest. It's less daunting for the children, you see, especially the younger ones.'

Karen nodded. 'I understand. And I'm glad you told me. I shall bear it in mind in future.'

'I hope I haven't offended you, dear?' Denise said, looking worried. 'And it certainly wasn't meant as a criticism of you or your work. You have a natural gift when dealing with the children. I've seen for myself how they respond to you and how much you care about them. In fact, Gray Woods was telling me about your idea to bring Ian and Kevin together. He was most enthusiastic, too.'

'Of course I'm not offended! I'm only too glad of any pointers, Denise,' she replied sincerely. 'One of the joys of working here is how much I feel I am learning. Oh, you can read textbooks and case studies but the only way to *really* learn how to help a child is through working with them.'

'Good!' Denise said happily, obviously reassured that she hadn't caused offence. 'It's no wonder everyone agrees how well you've fitted in. You have the right attitude and that makes all the difference. So, shall we see if any of the little horrors have arrived yet?'

Karen laughed as Denise rolled her eyes as she led the way to the door. From the noise coming from Reception, the children were not only there but eager to get started! She said hello to the mothers as they entered the large playroom which they would be using for the session.

Helena Harper-Ward, the little girl whose parents had

been so worried about her, was there with her nanny, Francesca. Karen had a word with the younger woman when she saw how nervous she looked.

'This is all very informal, Francesca, so I don't want you to worry. It isn't some sort of test or anything like that. We'll just play with the children and encourage them to speak to us and to each other.'

'I see. But 'Elena's parents, they will want to know everything she does.' Francesca rolled expressively dark eyes. 'They expect so much...of me and the little one. She is only a baby. *Sí?*'

Karen nodded although she knew it wouldn't be diplomatic to say too much. In her view, the Harper-Wards would be best advised to take a more relaxed approach.

She ushered Francesca into the room and closed the door, thinking back to what Denise had said to her. Maybe she should learn to relax more and adopt a less rigid approach? And if she did, then maybe her life would pick up? But at what cost?

She sighed as she went to sort out a fight which had erupted between two small boys who both wanted to play with the same toy car. Ifs, ands and buts weren't guarantees that she wouldn't be making a mistake, though, were they? Maybe it was a question of trust, but was she capable of trusting herself—or anyone else, for that matter?

Unbidden, a picture of Nick's smiling face came to mind and for some reason she didn't try to erase it this time.

'No! *Cara mia*, no. *Birichina!*'

Karen looked round and smiled as she saw Francesca admonishing her small charge for some minor misdemeanour. It had been a hectic morning, but it had gone extremely well; both she and Denise were pleased with what they had achieved. Helena, for instance, had had great fun playing with the other children although she had shown a marked reluctance to speak. It was a huge shock, therefore, when Karen heard the little girl break into a torrent of rapid Italian as she ran to her nanny.

Karen waited until Helena was once more happily absorbed in her game—pouring orange juice for the rest of the children from a toy teapot—before she had a word with Francesca. Drawing the Italian girl to one side, she set about finding out what was going on.

'I couldn't help noticing that Helena spoke to you in Italian just now, Francesca,' she observed quietly. 'She seemed to have no difficulty making herself understood.'

'Ah, no! The little one speaks so well in Italian.' Francesca shrugged. 'There is no problem there. The trouble lies with 'er English. *Sí?*'

'Oh, yes. I understand!' Karen laughed softly as everything suddenly slipped into place. 'I imagine that you speak Italian to Helena quite often, then?'

'But, yes.' Francesca looked momentarily unsure. 'You think that is wrong?'

'Not at all,' Karen hastened to assure her. 'But it could explain why Helena is so reluctant to speak English. Because you two spend so much time together, she *thinks* in Italian which means it is harder for her to speak in her own language.'

Francesca looked shocked. 'But 'Elena's parents will be so *angry* with me when they find out. Day after day they ask me about 'er progress, 'ave I done this or that with 'er. They will tell me to leave if they find out it is all my fault!'

Karen shook her head. 'It isn't your fault. And it most certainly isn't something we can't put right, either.' She smiled encouragingly. 'Mrs Harper-Ward mentioned something about a list of activities she expects you to do with Helena after kindergarten; is that right?'

'*Sí!*' Francesca rolled her eyes. 'Reading, writing, even the numbers. They do not seem to understand that 'Elena is only a baby!'

'She is only young but reading to her, for instance, is invaluable. It means that she not only hears the words being spoken out loud and understands them but she will start to recognise the letters…'

Karen paused as she saw the guilty expression on Francesca's face. It only took her a moment to work out what was wrong. 'You've been reading to her in Italian, haven't you?'

Francesca nodded unhappily. 'The books 'er mother left for us are so dull! Educational books, Mrs 'Arper-Ward called them, but the stories…! I 'ave some picture books which I brought from my 'ome so I read them to 'Elena instead. And she loves them,' she added defensively. 'She knows all the stories by 'eart now.'

Karen just managed not to laugh out loud. No wonder the poor child had no inclination to speak English when for most of the day all she heard was Italian! However, she had to make Francesca understand how important it was that Helena be encouraged to speak her own language.

'I do understand, Francesca. My advice to you is to take Helena to your local library and enrol her in the children's section, then you can borrow any amount of wonderful picture books. Then I'm afraid the Italian stories will have to go for now. Helena is getting confused by trying to think and speak in two languages at once, you see.'

'I understand. And you will not report me to 'er parents?' Francesca asked worriedly. 'I like this job. Mr and Mrs 'Arper-Ward are never at 'ome and I love little 'Elena like my own child.'

And that was where the real problem lay, Karen thought as she reassured the nanny that she wouldn't mention what

had been going on unless Helena's parents specifically
asked her. If Helena's parents spent more time with her
rather than working out rotas and delegating responsibility
to the child's nanny, then there wouldn't *be* a problem!
Still, it was good to have got to the root of the trouble and
she was confident that Francesca would follow her advice
so things should work out.

The session came to an end at last. Karen helped Denise
clear up before they sat down and discussed what progress
the children had made. Denise laughed out loud when
Karen told her about Helena.

'Imagine that! You need to be a detective sometimes to
get to the root of a problem, don't you? Still, fingers
crossed things will go OK from now on.'

Denise sobered as she handed Karen a note. 'There was
a message for you from Gray Woods, by the way. He said
to tell you that he's had a word with Ian's parents about
your idea of getting Ian and Kevin together and they are
all for it. Evidently, the tumour isn't responding as everyone hoped and Gray doesn't think that an operation will be
feasible.'

'Oh, no! Does that mean what I think it does?' Karen
asked in concern.

'Unfortunately.' Denise sighed sadly. 'The general con-
sensus is that Ian has a few months left at the most so that's
why his parents want to do everything possible to make
sure he enjoys them. They believe that it would really help
him to have another boy his age to talk to.'

'Then I'll see if I can set it up. Obviously, I need to ask
permission from Kevin's parents and see what Kevin himself thinks about the idea...' She tailed off and sighed. 'I
hope it isn't asking too much of him. Ian is obviously ill
so maybe it would upset Kevin.'

'See what he says, then take it from there,' Denise advised. 'Kevin's due here on Monday afternoon, I believe, so maybe you could mention it to him *and* his parents then.'

'I can just imagine what his father is going to say!' Karen declared, wondering if she were mad to have suggested the idea in the first place.

She was still worrying about it when she went for her lunch and didn't even notice the man coming into the building as she crossed the foyer. It was only when she heard footsteps behind her that she looked round and felt her heart surge as she saw Nick. For a moment the rush of pleasure she felt on seeing him made it impossible to move and by the time she had recovered the use of her legs he was standing in front of her.

He smiled at her, his eyes so dark that her pulse started playing hopscotch, bobbing up and down. Crazy though it sounded, she knew that he was as pleased to see her as she was to see him and the realisation started to melt the ice which had encased her heart since Paul's defection.

'Hi, there! Are you just on your way to lunch?'

'I...erm...yes.' Karen cleared her throat as she heard the husky note in her voice. However, it was hard to behave naturally when he was looking at her as though Christmas and his birthday had both come at once!

She looked down at her feet, then tried again, striving for the cool, calm approach which had been so easy to adopt once upon a time. 'How did the conference go?'

'Fine. There was some interesting stuff and I enjoyed it but it's good to be back.' His voice dropped, its tone playing havoc with every nerve in her body. 'It gets very lonely being in a hotel room all on your own of a night. You really miss the people who are important to you.'

Karen couldn't think of anything to say to that and mercifully Nick filled the silence with a soft laugh. 'It looks great, Karen.'

He took a step back and treated her to a long and very thorough scrutiny. Karen felt her cheeks redden as she suddenly remembered that she was wearing the T-shirt he had given her.

'We had a group session for tinies today,' she hurriedly explained. 'I wanted to wear something cheerful.'

'Well, it fits the bill perfectly.' He gave her a quizzical smile. 'Do I take it that the session went well? There's a definite sparkle in your eyes today. In fact, I can't recall seeing you looking so pleased with life.'

'Oh, that's probably because I've just solved a problem which has been puzzling me,' she said, quickly launching into the tale of Helena and Francesca before he could start making any—wrong!—assumptions. If there was a sparkle in her eyes then it had nothing to do with his sudden appearance, she told herself sternly, then inwardly sighed.

She *was* pleased to see him and lying to herself wouldn't make a scrap of difference. Nick was kind and caring and fun to be with. In fact, he was everything that Denise had said he was. So why not accept that and treat him accordingly rather than keep trying to cast him in the role of villain? Perhaps the real root of the trouble she had in dealing with him was the fact that she didn't try to treat him like everyone else. So...

From now on she would be friendly and approachable, as congenial towards him as he was towards her, and she would see if that worked. Treat Nick as just another friend and colleague and *that* was what he would become!

Determined to follow her own sensible advice, she awarded him a warm smile. 'I was just on my way to lunch; are you coming?'

'I'd love to.' He pressed the button to summon the lift, then grinned at her. 'Letting your hair down?'

She frowned. 'Sorry?'

He laughed softly as they stepped into the lift and the doors closed. 'Rapunzel, Rapunzel, let down your hair... You know how it goes.'

Karen laughed dutifully although she couldn't deny the flicker of alarm she felt. 'Yes, I know!' She deliberately pretended not to understand him. 'And, no, I have no intention of letting down my hair. This T-shirt is enough of an image change for one day, thank you!'

'And very nice it looks too, as I said.' Nick didn't pursue it, smoothly changing the subject to one of the lectures he had attended at the conference. Karen was glad but that didn't mean she wasn't on edge.

Had Nick been asking if she was willing now to let people get closer to her? And if so, why? Because *he* wanted to get to know her better? But where would that lead?

Karen sighed as they reached their floor and headed towards the canteen. She would go mad if she kept going round in circles, asking endless questions like that! She had to stick to her decision to treat Nick the same as everyone else.

She shot a glance at him as she picked up a plate of salad, felt her pulse skitter before she brought it firmly under control. If she had to remind herself a hundred times an hour, then it would be worth it if it worked!

'I think it's a great idea.'

Nick sat back in his seat and smiled at her. Karen had been telling him about her plans to introduce Ian and Kevin and it was obvious that he approved.

'I thought so. Both boys desperately need someone of their own age to talk to because they are lonely.' She frowned. 'You don't think it would be too traumatic for Kevin, though? He might not have seen anyone who is so ill before.'

'I think it's something you need to consider. Perhaps if you have a word with his head teacher and see what he says,' Nick suggested thoughtfully. 'It sounds as though the poor lad doesn't get much encouragement at home so his teacher might be able to give you more of an insight into how Kevin might react.'

'That's an excellent idea! Thanks.' Karen smiled her delight. She saw Nick's eyes darken and her breath caught as she saw the expression they held before he looked down at his plate.

The very air seemed suddenly charged with emotion even though she wasn't sure what was going on. Nick had looked as though something momentous had happened to him yet she had no idea what it could be. It was a relief when Hugh Derbyshire suddenly appeared and interrupted them.

'Sorry to butt in but I wanted to remind you about that meeting with Martyn Lennard this afternoon, Nick. I'm going to be tied up in theatre so if you could stand in for me, I'd be eternally grateful.'

'Sure. No problem, Hugh. I hadn't forgotten. Three o'clock, wasn't it?'

Nick grinned wryly as the consultant moved away. 'Hugh hates meetings. He delegates me to go whenever he can. In his view, it's a waste of time which would be far better spent working with our patients.'

'An-and how do you feel about them?' Karen asked softly. She shot a wary glance at Nick but his face gave nothing away. He looked relaxed and at ease and there was no sign of the tension which had been so apparent just moments before. It made her wonder if she'd imagined it, but it was hard to accept that.

She forced herself to concentrate as she realised that he was still speaking. Maybe it would be better to forget all about it, in fact. She certainly didn't want to add any more questions to that seemingly inexhaustible list!

'I get as impatient as Hugh does but these meetings are a necessary evil. So much is down to funding nowadays and I am quite prepared to fight our corner if it means we get the extra money we need.'

'That sounds as though you have something planned. Are you trying to get a new project off the ground?' Karen queried, hearing the determination in his voice. There was no doubt that Nick would fight to the end if he believed in something passionately enough and she felt a warm glow inside her as once again it struck her how much he cared about what he did.

'We are hoping to extend the ENT ward. The number of cases we are seeing is increasing yearly and we are having to turn children away or refer them to other hospitals because we can't cope.' He shrugged. 'I'm not decrying what other hospitals do, but Lizzie's is a centre of excellence and that applies especially to ENT work. The more children who get the chance to be treated here, the better.'

'I understand. And I'm sure that most parents would agree and want the best for their children, too. It would be great if you could get the extra funding, Nick,' she said enthusiastically.

'It certainly would!' He grinned back at her. 'It seems we are in accord on that even though it *could* have a knock-on effect for your department, Karen.'

She laughed at the rueful note in his voice. 'Oh, I'm sure we would cope somehow! So long as the children are helped, then that's all that matters, isn't it?'

'Yes.' He reached over and squeezed her hand. 'That's all any of us aim to do at the end of the day, make sure these kids' lives are improved.'

Karen bit her lip as she felt a tingling sensation ripple

through her fingers. Nick's hand was so warm and strong as it gripped hers. It made her suddenly feel safe and secure, as though there was no need to be scared any more. It was such a long time since she had felt that way, too.

Her eyes rose to his and she felt her heartbeat quicken. She could see herself reflected in Nick's eyes, tiny twin images of her face mirrored in their depths. It made her feel as though somehow he had absorbed her very essence.

Had he? Could she let him? Could she find the courage to share with him her innermost fears and dreams, entrust him with her deepest secrets? That was the worst thing about what Paul had done; he had destroyed her ability to trust anyone. But maybe the time would come when she could relearn how to do it? All she needed was to find the right man…someone she could trust.

She withdrew her hand and stood up. Nick didn't try to stop her leaving. He just looked at her with eyes which held a world of tenderness. 'I think I mentioned to you about the birthday party for my father this Saturday. Won't you change your mind and come, Karen?'

She took a tiny breath but the air seemed to fill every bit of her lungs until it felt as though they would explode from the pressure. Even her heart felt as though it were being squeezed tightly because she could feel the blood pumping in and out of it. It was such a huge step and she couldn't be sure that it wasn't a mistake but she wanted to take it. Suddenly, she knew that more than anything else she wanted to break free of the past, if only she had the courage to do so!

'I…' She had to stop and breathe out before she could continue and even then her voice sounded strained. 'I would like that, Nick. Thank you.'

'Then I'll pick you up around seven, if that's all right?' His tone was even but she heard the gravelly note it held and knew that he wasn't unmoved by her acceptance. Did Nick see it as a huge step too? Or was he unaware of what it had cost her? She could convince herself that he felt either way because she just didn't know!

Karen gave him her address, then hurriedly left the canteen and spent the rest of the day concentrating on her work. It was far safer. If she let herself think about what she had agreed to, then panic would set in.

A date with Nick Bentley.

Karen stared into the mirror, seeing the apprehension in her grey eyes. It was Saturday evening and seven o'clock was approaching—fast!

She took a deep breath and squared her shoulders. She wasn't going to chicken out. She was going to go through with it. She was going to get herself ready and behave as though nothing out of the ordinary was happening. It wasn't, because there must be hundreds—thousands!—of women all across the country getting ready for an evening out. It was just that it was such a...a leap of faith for her, so was she really and truly ready to take it? No way!

Dropping her lipstick onto the shelf which doubled as a dressing table, Karen ran to the phone. She would call Nick and explain that she was very sorry but unfortunately she wouldn't be able to make it after all. She snatched up the receiver as she quickly rehearsed her excuse.

Flu? No, that would need a week off work to recover. How about a chill? Or maybe a headache...a *migraine* with sickness and flashing lights and distorted vision—the whole works. Brilliant!

Her finger hovered over the buttons ready to dial before it hit her that she didn't know his number. She dropped the receiver back onto its rest with a moan of dismay, then dropped to her knees to hunt the phone directory from un-

der the bed, which had been the only nook she'd been able
to find to store it.

She snapped it open, mumbling under her breath as she
flicked through the As at a rate of knots, then slowed as
she came to the Bs. She was conscious that the minutes
were flying past and she didn't want to run the risk of Nick
leaving home to collect her before she could stop him.

'Barnes, Bartlett, Benjamin, Benson...' she reeled off before she reached the section for Bentley.

The doorbell suddenly pealed and Karen froze. It
couldn't be him! It was far too early! She pressed a hand
to her thundering heart as she knelt beside the bed. Maybe
it was a double-glazing salesman? Or one of those brave
souls from some religious sect? Or a neighbour wanting to
borrow a cup of sugar? If she stayed quite still and didn't
make a sound, then they would go away.

The bell rang again, with a touch of impatience. Karen
squeaked in fright. She pressed a hand to her lips but the
damage had been done. There was a sharp rap on her door
accompanied by a verbal summons this time.

'Karen? It's me, Nick. Come on, open up!'

'I...I'm coming.' Boiling oil and thumbscrews would
have got the words out sounding more enthusiastic than
they did as they issued from her lips. Karen stumbled to
her feet and made her reluctant way to the door. Nick's
brows rose as she opened it as wide as a nervous spinster
would have recommended.

'Aren't you going to invite me in?' he asked smoothly.

'I...erm...well, yes, I suppose so.'

Karen fumbled with the chain and let him in. He walked
to the centre of the room and looked around. His gaze
immediately homed in on the open telephone directory before he treated her to a look which brought the colour to
her face.

'Did I interrupt you making a call?' he asked in that same silky tone which was starting to grate.

Karen took a deep breath and tightened the belt on her robe. She felt at a distinct disadvantage dressed in her bath-robe with her hair hanging loose. However, maybe she could make it work to her advantage with a bit of luck?

'I was just trying to find your number, actually.' She pressed a limp hand to her forehead and closed her eyes. 'I'm afraid that I'm going to have to cry off tonight, Nick. I've got this terrible headache, you see. Well, it's more like a migraine, really...flashing lights, distorted vision...the lot.'

'Really? Then don't you think you should be lying down?'

His tone was sympathetic enough to encourage her to squint at him through her lashes and she was reassured by what she saw. There didn't seem to be a hint of suspicion on his face so maybe he believed she was telling the truth.

'You're probably right.' She managed a brave little smile, playing her part to the utmost. Frankly, she deserved an Oscar for this performance! 'I'll take a couple of aspirins and lie down. Hopefully, it will help.'

She turned towards the door, remembering at the last second to move with the slowness of one whose head felt as though it were in imminent danger of departing her body. 'I'm so sorry to have to call our evening off. And sorrier still that you've had a wasted journey...' she began.

'Oh, it hasn't been wasted.' Nick's hand was firm as it closed around her arm as he steered her across the room. He stopped beside the bed and whipped back the covers. His smile was tinged with sympathy and a whole lot of other things as he looked into her shocked eyes.

'You didn't think I would desert you in your hour of

need, did you, Karen?' He gently pushed her backwards so
that she sank onto the mattress, then shook his head.

'Of course not. No, I'll stay right here and look after you
until you're feeling better. And I won't let you try and talk
me out of it!'

CHAPTER EIGHT

'I'M SO pleased you could come, my dear. You're very welcome.'

'Thank you.' Karen fixed a smile into place as she responded to the genuine warmth of the greeting. However, that didn't mean she wasn't still smarting...

'We're lucky that she made it here. When I arrived to pick her up she had the most awful headache. She did think it was a migraine at first, in fact. How do you feel now, Karen?' Nick's tone was just right: kind, considerate, *sympathetic*. It obviously convinced his mother because Mrs Bentley was instantly concerned.

'Oh, how dreadful! Are you sure you should have come if you aren't feeling well? I hope you didn't let Nick talk you into it.' Mrs Bentley shot an adoring look at her son. 'He can be so very *persuasive* at times that it's hard to say no to him!'

Karen laughed dutifully. If she hadn't done then she might have been tempted to tell Nick's mother exactly what she thought of her beloved son! However, bearing in mind that this was meant to be a family occasion, that didn't seem wise. She contented herself with the truth even though she had to force the words out through gritted teeth.

'No, I'm fine. Honestly.'

'Good.' Mrs Bentley patted Karen's arm, then turned to her son. 'Get Karen a drink, will you, darling? Your father's due back from his club any moment and I want to make sure everyone has a drink to toast him with. You'll find the rest of the gang in the conservatory so make your way there. I shall bring him through as soon as he arrives.'

'Of course.' Nick turned to Karen as his mother hurried away. 'What would you like? Maybe it would be better to avoid anything alcoholic in case your headache comes back?'

Karen glowered at him. 'A glass of wine would be fine. Thank you.'

He smiled at her, his mouth curling upwards as he studied her frosty expression. 'Well, if you're sure, then wine it is.' He pointed towards a door at the far end of the hall. 'If you go through there you'll find the conservatory. I'll bring the drinks through.'

He headed in the opposite direction but for a moment Karen didn't move as she glared at his retreating back. Nick had played her at her own game, making out that he had believed she'd been too ill to go out! Short of bodily ejecting him from her flat, Karen hadn't stood a chance of getting rid of him…as he'd made it clear.

He had dispensed tea, sympathy and aspirin in equal amounts and with a concern which had made her want to do something drastic. Her pleas that she would be fine and that she didn't want to spoil his evening, that his mother must be wondering where he had got to and his father would be disappointed, had fallen on deaf ears. When Nick had announced that he intended to stay and play the ministering angel he had meant it!

In the end, Karen had caved in. Not even trying to hide her annoyance, she had announced that her headache was gone. Nick had silkily offered to wait outside while she got dressed, which she had done in record time. Her best black dress had been dragged over her head, her hair coiled into a loose chignon, her feet slipped into the highest pair of strappy sandals she'd been able to find. It had been a small consolation when she had seen his eyes widen as she had stepped out of the door, an even bigger one when she had discovered that the high heels meant she was a good couple of inches taller than he was. Good! He'd wanted her to go with him so he would just have to lump it if he didn't like the fact that she towered over him!

However, if he *had* been disconcerted, then he'd not let it show. He had been at his most urbane as they had driven to his parents' home—a massive house on the bank of the Thames—oozing sympathy until Karen had wanted to scream if she'd heard another solicitous word. In fact, she still might, she decided, spinning round on her heel as he disappeared through one of the numerous doors which led off from the hall. She might just let rip and have a good hard scream because it could only make her feel better. How did Nick manage to make her feel like *this* with so little effort?

She pushed open the door she had been directed to and found herself in a short hallway which led to the conservatory. The lights were on inside it and she could see several dozen people milling about. She glanced back, suddenly nervous about walking into a room full of strangers on her own. Contrary though it was, she suddenly wished that Nick were there.

She sighed, realising that once again she was wavering between wanting to be with him and treating him like a carrier of the Black Death. Where Nick was concerned there were no hard and fast rules, it seemed.

'You must be Karen.'

Karen looked round, summoning a tentative smile for the woman who had come out of the conservatory to meet her. 'I am, but how did you know?'

'Oh, because I've heard such a lot about you, of course!'

The woman smiled warmly as she held out her hand. 'I'm Melanie Bentley, Jamie's mother.'

'It's nice to meet you,' Karen replied rather stiffly, wondering why she found it so hard to respond to the friendly greeting. She took rapid stock of Nick's sister-in-law as they shook hands, her heart sinking as she saw that Melanie was every bit as beautiful as she had expected her to be.

Melanie was small and delicate-looking, her long blonde hair caught back by tortoiseshell combs from her heart-shaped face. Her skin was porcelain fine, her features dainty and perfectly formed. She was wearing a flowing dress in layers of misty green which only added to the ethereal image of feminine charm.

Karen felt like a giant standing beside her in three-inch spike heels and rued the fact that she had worn them. However, there was little she could do except try to carry the meeting off with aplomb.

'Nick's fetching me a drink,' she said quickly, realising that the other woman was waiting for her to say something.

'Then we may as well go back inside the conservatory and sit down.' Melanie gave a melodic laugh as she put a slender hand on Karen's arm. 'Hugh's getting me a drink and you know what it's like when they get together!'

Karen laughed dutifully as Melanie led the way into the conservatory. She had *no* idea what Hugh and Nick were like when they got together because she'd only ever seen them both in work, and the thought irked her. However, it seemed pointless worrying about it so she concentrated on fitting names to faces as Melanie introduced her to the rest of the guests. Her head was soon spinning with the effort of trying to keep track so that it was a relief when a familiar little figure suddenly appeared and ran over to hug her.

Karen hugged Jamie back, then turned to his mother. 'He

looks really well. Obviously, he's recovered from his operation.'

Melanie put a loving hand on her son's head as he went to her side. 'He has. I feel so silly the way I worried about it. I should have known he would be all right because he had the best doctor in the world taking care of him.'

She looked towards the door. Karen felt her heart sink as she saw Nick coming in with Hugh Derbyshire. It didn't take a genius to work out what Melanie had meant. Hadn't she seen the loving expression in the other woman's eyes as she had looked at Nick?

She turned away as the two men came to join them, afraid that her own expression might be equally revealing. How did Nick feel about his beautiful sister-in-law, though? It was a question she had the right neither to ask nor expect an answer to and that seemed to hurt all the more. Crazy to think that she had wanted to keep Nick at arm's length all this time and that now she wanted to know everything about him!

'Here you go, white wine and soda.' He handed her a glass, smiling as she stared dumbly at the drink. 'I thought it might be better for the headache than straight wine.'

Suddenly, his teasing started to get her down. Her head came up and she stared him straight in the eyes. 'I didn't have a headache. It was a lie.'

'I know.' He took a sip of his own drink although his eyes didn't leave hers. 'You had a severe attack of nerves which is just as painful, sweetheart.'

Sweetheart? Karen absorbed the gentle endearment as Hugh claimed his attention. Melanie joined in the conversation and the three of them were soon chatting away. Karen didn't hear a word they said, however, because her mind was completely taken up by those ten letters. They skittered around inside her head, singly, doubly, then back in formation: sweetheart. How strange that she had never realised before just how beautiful that word could sound.

'He's here! Get ready everyone!'

Karen jumped as Nick's mother called out to warn them that Mr Bentley had arrived. Suddenly, the conservatory lights went out, plunging them into darkness. Karen's pulse leapt as she felt a warm hand fold around hers. Nick drew her against his side as he whispered in her ear.

'Dad will have a fit when he discovers what's going on.'

The blackness had robbed her of one of her senses so maybe that was why the others suddenly began to work overtime. Nick was so near that she could feel the warmth of his breath on her cheek, smell the scent of his skin, hear the vibrations from his voice pulsating in her ear...

She wasn't sure who moved first or if they both moved together. She simply turned her head and found that he had turned his. Their lips touched, tasted, clung for one second...two...then separated. He didn't say a word and neither did she. There was no need. It had been all there encoded in that kiss. Nick wanted her and she wanted him. The realisation both thrilled and scared her because she wasn't sure she was ready to cope with what it could mean.

'Surprise! Happy birthday, darling.'

The lights went on and a great cheer went up. Karen blinked, feeling dazed. She glanced at Nick and could tell that he felt the same way even though he was trying his best not to show it.

A feeling of intense warmth flowed through her. It was as though a dam had burst and all the fear had been swept away. How could she be scared when Nick had doubts of his own? Surely it just proved that he was as vulnerable as she was and that he would never, ever hurt her?

The thought flowed through her head in a millisecond. It was there and gone before he had turned and smiled at her. She smiled back, not even trying to hide how happy she felt.

'Karen.' He started to speak, then stopped. Maybe he was having difficulty understanding what was going on, but she wasn't! She had been set free from the past thanks to one little kiss—not just any kiss, however, but Nick's kiss. That was what had made all the difference.

'Let's get out of here, shall we?'

He recovered fast, taking firm hold of her hand as he pushed his way through the crowd. Everyone was so caught up in what was happening that they didn't seem to notice them leaving. Nick let the conservatory door slam shut then turned to her and there was a glitter in his eyes which made her heart race.

'I don't think we'll be missed for half an hour, do you?' he grated, his eyes tracing her face as though he were trying to drink in each tiny line and pore.

'Your father...?' she began, then shook her head. 'No, I don't suppose so.'

She could hear the expectant note in her voice and knew that Nick had heard it too. When he pulled her into his arms, she didn't even think of resisting. She knew what was going to happen, of course, but it was what she wanted as much as he did. His lips were fierce as they took hers, yet tender too. It was such a devastating combination that it moved her to tears.

He drew back and looked at her with eyes so gentle that her heart opened. 'Will you tell me about it, Karen? Tell me who hurt you so badly?'

'Yes.' Maybe she shouldn't have agreed but suddenly she no longer needed to keep it a secret. It was Paul who had been in the wrong, not her. She felt a deep sense of relief that at last everything would come out into the open. It was time to let go of the past and start living again.

'I...' She stopped and looked round as a burst of laughter issued from the conservatory. Nick gave her a rueful smile as he caught hold of her hand and lifted it to his lips to gently kiss her knuckles.

'Here isn't the best place to talk, is it? Let's go into the library. We won't be disturbed there.'

He led her along the hall and opened a door at the far side of the house. Karen took a long look around as she went into the room, loving what she saw. It was a room to relax in, to be at peace in, and its magic immediately began to work on her.

'Why don't you sit down? The sofa's very comfortable. How about another drink? You didn't get chance to finish the last one.'

Oddly enough, it was Nick who seemed keyed up as he waved her towards one of the sofas, then opened a cabinet and took out some glasses. Karen frowned as she sat down, wondering what was wrong with him until it hit her that he was nervous—for *her*!

'I don't want another drink, thank you,' she told him softly, her heart swelling at the thought.

'Sure?' He turned and she could see the worry in his eyes. She shook her head, a gentle smile playing about her mouth as she looked steadily at him.

'Quite sure.'

He suddenly grimaced. 'I don't want one either. I just feel so...well, so screwed up about this, Karen. I don't know if I should have asked you to tell me what happened because I don't want to hurt you. That's the last thing I want, in fact!'

'You aren't hurting me, Nick.' She looked down, studying the pattern on the old, faded rug because she needed something to focus on rather than his anxious face. She had to keep this in proportion and not let her imagination run

away with at her. All right, so that kiss had been a kind of
catalyst for her, but she couldn't be sure that it had meant
anything to him. One kiss didn't make a *relationship* or
anything else for that matter. If she told Nick what had
gone on then it was for her sake and she mustn't go expecting too much from him.

'It's way past time I dealt with what happened to me,'
she began softly. 'I've been bottling it all up and trying not
to think about it.' She gave a rueful laugh. 'However, it
hasn't achieved very much apart from spurring me on to
change jobs!'

'So your decision to move to London was prompted by
what happened to you?' He shrugged but she could tell that
he was simply trying to keep the mood light. 'Would I be
right in assuming that it was a broken relationship?'

'Yes. I'd say how did you guess, only it's not that difficult, is it?' She sighed. 'It's a familiar enough tale, I expect, only it's different when it happens to you. No one
likes to know that she's been made a fool of.'

'Was that what happened to you, Karen?' He came and
sat beside her, taking her hand to link his fingers through
hers.

She felt a lump come to her throat and had to swallow
before she could answer. 'Yes. I fell in love, you see,
thought that he loved me but he didn't. I was just a...a bit
of fun to Paul, someone to play around with, to...to sleep
with...'

She couldn't go on. She was afraid to look at Nick because she had no idea what his reaction would be. Would
he think she was a fool? Would he be disgusted even?
There was no way of knowing. Yet she knew in her heart
how important his opinion was to her.

'So how did you find out that this guy had been using
you?' His voice grated, but not with disgust. Karen heard

the anger it held and knew at once that it was for the way
she had been treated. Nick was angry for *her* sake and it
was so wonderful to know that. It helped to give her the
courage to tell him the worst part of the whole sordid tale.

'When his wife turned up at my home one night and told
me how much she despised me for what I was doing to her
and her children.' She felt Nick grip her hand and gripped
his back, needing his strength to help her continue.

'I…I had no idea that Paul was married up till then. I
don't think anyone did know and that isn't just an excuse.
He'd moved from Brighton to the hospital where I worked
and nobody knew much about him, although on the surface
he was very open and charming.'

'Hell!' The exclamation was bitten out. She had the feeling that Nick instantly regretted expressing his feeling so
bluntly but she didn't mind. She had been so ashamed and
embarrassed that she hadn't been able to tell anyone about
what had happened, not even her parents. It was such a
relief to be able to share it with someone who cared.

'Hell, indeed!' she said lightly. 'I was completely taken
in by him, you see. He was handsome, witty, fun to be with
and all the nurses were crazy about him. I couldn't believe
it when he asked me out when he could have had his pick.'

She gave a tinkly little laugh but she heard the bitterness
it held even though she'd tried to disguise it. 'It turned out
that Paul saw me as a challenge, you see. I had a reputation
for being choosy about who I went out with and that just
increased my appeal so far as Paul was concerned. Maybe
he thought that he scored extra points for sleeping with a
virgin.'

Nick swore softly. He got up abruptly and went to the
window. 'So what happened once you found out that he
had been stringing you along?'

'Pretty much what you would expect. I confronted him

with what had happened and he just laughed. He seemed
to think it highly amusing that his wife had seen fit to warn
me off. Evidently, she had stayed behind to sell their house,
which is why they weren't living together.'

She shrugged, wishing that he would turn round so that
she could see his face and maybe gauge his reaction to what
she was saying. 'She came to visit him and found a letter
I'd written to him. It wasn't the first time he'd been un-
faithful to her, apparently, and it probably won't be the last,
but they are still together I believe, so that's one consolation. At least I can't be accused of breaking up a marriage
and leaving two small children fatherless!'

'You weren't to blame for any of it, Karen! You must
know that?'

He came striding back and stopped in front of her. His
face was set into grim lines, his black eyes ablaze with an
inner fire, but it was a fire which had ignited on *her* behalf.
Nick wasn't angry about what she had done but because of
what had been done to her!

Tears filled her eyes again as she realised it and she heard
him utter something harsh as he pulled her to her feet.
'Don't, Karen! You mustn't blame yourself. It wasn't your
fault!'

He took her face between his hands, holding her so that
he could look into her eyes. 'You were the innocent victim
in all this, sweetheart.'

There it was again, that same endearment which might
mean something or could mean nothing. Karen had no idea
which it was and tried to smile but it was a poor effort.
Nick groaned as he pulled her towards him...

He suddenly stopped. A frown pleated his brows as his
gaze swept up, then down to her feet. Before Karen had
time to realise what was happening, he'd knelt down and

lifted her right foot onto his bent knee while he deftly un-
fastened the narrow ankle strap on her black suede sandal.

His fingers caressed her instep, then the back of her heel
as he slid the sandal off her foot and placed it to one side
before turning his attention to her other foot.

Karen bit her lip as once again she felt the caressing
touch of his fingers slide over her arch and heel before her
left foot was gently planted on the floor. Nick rose to his
feet and grinned wickedly as he carried on with his aborted
mission, pulling her swiftly into his arms.

'That's better,' he murmured. 'Now you are a perfect fit!'

Karen didn't have time to reply before his mouth found
hers, settling so gently, so delicately over hers that it felt
more like a benediction than a kiss. People spoke of healing
hands but this was even better because Nick had healing
lips!

The last remnants of pain seeped from her as he set about
kissing away all the hurt and heartache. For a while she
was so involved in being healed that it was impossible to
do anything more than accept what was happening. Then
slowly, the sweetness of his mouth began to stir feelings
inside her which she had believed were gone for ever. At
first she resisted them because she was afraid to trust her
own instincts. However, it was impossible to deny them for
long.

Her lips parted on a gentle sigh and she felt Nick stiffen.
Maybe he was surprised by her response because there was
a moment when it seemed that he would pull away and her
heart cried out in fear. She twined her arms around his
neck, letting her fingers slide into the silky hair at his nape
while she urged him closer, and he didn't resist!

Karen felt her heart bubble with joy as his tongue slid
into her mouth and mated with hers. It was a dance as old
as time but they danced it so well together. Each sweep of

his tongue was mirrored by hers, each nibbling, tasting, savouring of lips was mimicked by the other. It felt as though they had kissed like this a thousand times yet it was the first time and that made it all the more special and to be cherished.

When they drew apart, she knew that Nick felt as shaken as she did, that *he* hadn't expected that explosion of passion, let alone the skill they had discovered together to deal with it.

He rested his forehead against hers and she could feel him trembling. 'I wish I could think of something better to say but all I can come up with is wow! You are some kisser, Karen Young.'

'So are you, Nick Bentley.'

Karen smiled, wondering how it was possible to tease and be teased when something so momentous had happened. But that was what made Nick different, special. With Nick passion would be forever tempered by tenderness, desire by warmth, sorrow by joy. He could cross all the boundaries and not be afraid.

She knew that her eyes must be full of wonderment at the discovery yet she didn't try to hide it from him. He smiled as he cupped her cheek and his eyes were tender and full of everything she felt.

'I think we'd better get back to the festivities before they send out a search party,' he said softly, although his tone told her that he would have preferred to do something entirely different.

'We should,' she replied huskily, although she, too, wanted to say something else. However, it was too soon to ignore *all* the old rules, to forget *every* lesson she had learned. Next time she gave her heart to anyone then she had to be sure it wasn't a mistake and as yet she wasn't one hundred per cent certain. Ninety-nine per cent, maybe, but not that magical one hundred. Still, there was no need to rush.

She smiled as Nick escorted her back to the party. They had all the time in the world to get this right.

'Right, I'll leave you two to get acquainted. I'll come back for you in what...half an hour, shall we say, Kevin?'

Karen gave the boy a reassuring smile as he nodded. It was his first visit to see Ian and she knew that both boys were a little nervous. Funnily enough, it had been easier than she'd expected making the arrangements. Kevin's mother had brought him in for his appointment on that Monday afternoon a week ago and had readily given her permission. Karen had gained the distinct impression that Mrs Walters was only too keen to get the boy out of the house and these visits to see Ian would be the perfect op-portunity.

As for Kevin, he had seemed intrigued by the idea of meeting someone who shared his interests and had happily agreed to her suggestion. However, the final blessing had come from Kevin's teacher who had stated categorically that *anything* which would help the boy come out of his shell was worth a try. Strange how seemingly massive ob-stacles could be surmounted if one tried. But hadn't she discovered that in other areas of her life as well recently?

'Great, I was hoping to catch you. Denise said you were here. Are we still on for the cinema tonight?'

Karen felt her heart kick into overdrive as Nick appeared. 'Of course. I'm looking forward to it. I've been dying to see that new romantic comedy for ages.'

'I thought we were going to see that sci-fi movie?' Nick held up his hands as she opened her mouth and treated her to a wicked grin. 'OK. OK. You win but I shall expect some suitable form of recompense, you understand?'

'Mmm, I'm not sure I know what you mean, Dr Bentley. You may need to explain that...' she began, then gasped as he dropped a swift but exceedingly thorough kiss on her mouth.

'That was a taster for what I had in mind. Think about it! See you at seven.'

He went racing off towards the lift before she could reply. Karen smiled bemusedly as she headed for the office to have a word with Gray Woods and bring him up to date on the two boys' first meeting. In the week since the party, she and Nick had spent a lot of time together both in and out of work. They had been for walks in the park at lunchtime, for drinks after work of an evening. If it hadn't sounded odd in this high-tech age, she would have said that he was *courting* her, but she wasn't objecting.

She enjoyed being with him, enjoyed his company and the fact that he didn't try to push their relationship too far. She knew that he wanted her physically, but he hadn't made any attempt to get her into bed. She sensed that he was giving her time and she appreciated it.

It was working, too, because Nick not only made her feel good about herself but he made her believe that she had a future to look forward to, although whether that future would include him wasn't clear. She tried not to dwell on that too much, just took each day as it came, but she knew in her heart that she was keeping her fingers crossed. Maybe that one hundred per cent was *almost* within reach!

Karen went back to collect Kevin half an hour later and was thrilled when she glanced into the room and saw that the two boys were chatting away. Ian had been given a side room now because the effects of the drugs were making him feel very ill. His condition had deteriorated since she had first seen him but there was a definite sparkle in his eyes when she entered the room.

'Brill...look...brill!'

His speech was getting worse as the tumour expanded. However, it was obvious that he and Kevin had got along fine together.

Kevin's face was wreathed in smiles as he showed Karen the stack of magazines. 'Ian s-s-s-s-said I c-c-c-can borrow these!'

Karen was thrilled by his excitement and the fact that he had managed to say a whole sentence with relatively little trouble. 'Why, that's great! You'll be able to read them and then swop stories about which birds you've seen.'

Ian struggled to open his locker. 'Note...see.'

He held up a hardback notebook. Karen took it from him and flicked through the pages. She whistled softly when she saw that it contained a list of birds along with notes about the places and dates when Ian had seen them.

'This is amazing, Ian. What a huge number of birds you've seen,' she declared, carefully returning the precious book to the boy's locker.

'I...I'm g-g-g-going to do that,' Kevin declared. 'K-k-k-keep a lis-s-st.'

'That's a good idea. In fact, if I'm not mistaken I have a notebook in my office which would be just perfect. I'll give it to you before you leave, Kevin,' she offered immediately.

Kevin smiled with pleasure. He seemed like a different boy as they went down to her office. Karen found the notebook for him, then took him back to his father, her heart sinking as she saw how Kevin clammed up the minute he saw the man. She couldn't begin to imagine what the poor boy's home life must be like.

The time flew past after that. She had another session with Becky Dobbs which went very well. The little girl had been so buoyed up by her performance on the Karaoke machine that she had asked to join the school choir and been accepted.

Karen was thrilled and congratulated her warmly, brushing aside Mrs Dobbs' thanks for her input. However, she couldn't deny that it was a wonderful feeling to know that she had helped the girl achieve her dream.

This second success cast a rosy glow over the rest of the day. She didn't even mind Josie's teasing enquiry when they went for their break about why she was looking so happy and did it have anything to do with a *certain* doctor?

Karen took it all in her stride. So what if rumours about her and Nick were flying about the place? What did it matter so long as they were happy with the situation? She was and she thought that Nick was, so that was fine. She certainly wasn't going to let a bit of gossip spoil things!

On that positive note she worked through the rest of the afternoon. Denise had left early to visit her son so Karen collected her coat and locked up. She was just crossing the foyer when Nick hailed her and she stopped to let him catch her up. However, her welcoming smile quickly faded as she saw the look on his face.

'What's happened, Nick?' she demanded because it was obvious that something was wrong.

'It's Jamie,' he explained without any preamble. 'He's had to be readmitted. He's running a temperature and has enlarged glands in his neck. It looks very much as though he might have an infection and the implant will have to be removed.'

'Oh, no! But I thought he was getting on so well. He seemed fine when I saw him the other night,' she exclaimed in concern.

'I know. I can't understand it, frankly. It's extremely rare that the implant causes any problems. I certainly can't recall another case since I started working here.'

Karen could hear the anxiety in his voice and wished she could do something. She laid her hand on his arm but he didn't seem to notice.

'Anyway, I have to go. As luck would have it, Hugh is off today but I've left a message for him so, hopefully, he'll get back to me. I'm afraid this means we'll have to cancel tonight, but it can't be helped.' He shrugged. 'Mel's really upset, as you can imagine. She needs me to be here with her.'

'Yes, of course,' Karen said flatly. Nick didn't waste any more time as he hurried away. Why should he, though? Melanie needed him and that was what really mattered. Maybe he was just beginning to realise what Karen had suspected all along—that he felt more than just a *brotherly* attachment to the other woman?

She took a deep breath but it didn't help ease the knot of pain which had encircled her heart. It gripped it so hard that it seemed to be squeezing all the life and vitality out of her. Nick liked her and enjoyed her company, he even *desired* her, but it meant very little at the end of the day. She was just another in a long list of women who had fallen under his spell and she couldn't blame them or herself.

Nick was warm, caring, handsome and funny. He was everything a man should be and everything a woman could want. The pity of it was that there was only one woman *he* wanted, only one woman he *really* cared about. Maybe it was time that he faced up to that and told her. If he finally admitted to Melanie that he loved her, then everyone would be happy.

Well, maybe not *everyone*. She certainly wouldn't be!

CHAPTER NINE

THE next few days seemed to pass in a blur. Sometimes, Karen felt as though she were functioning on automatic pilot. She *said* and *did* all the right things but it was as though she wasn't really in control.

Nick was conspicuous by his absence and she didn't know whether to be glad or sorry. She heard via the grapevine that he was spending every spare minute with his nephew. Karen would have liked to visit the child but she decided it wouldn't be wise in case she ran into Nick.

Part of her wanted to see Nick and offer him her support but the other part of her was afraid. What did she really have to offer him? Surely Melanie was the only person who could provide what he needed at this difficult time. They could comfort each other and grow even closer through doing so.

That thought didn't help at all. She found it difficult to sleep at night with thinking about it all—about Nick and Melanie and the life they would make together. It left her feeling even more wretched, although she refused point-blank to work out why. Facing up to the truth, the whole truth—all one hundred per cent of it—was more than she could bear.

She left work at the end of another day feeling more depressed than she had felt in her whole life. The good weather had broken a few days earlier and the city was awash as rain swept through the streets. By the time Karen reached her flat she was soaked to the skin and shivering with cold. It didn't help to discover that the old water heater in the bathroom had broken down and that workmen laying new sewers in the area had cut through the electricity cables.

She spent a miserable night in the dark huddled up in bed trying to keep warm and woke the next morning with a runny nose and sore throat. To add insult to injury, her bus didn't turn up, so she got another soaking as she waited for the next one to arrive.

Denise took one look at her when she arrived at work and shook her head. 'You shouldn't be here! You look awful.'

'Thanks!' Karen tried to smile but her head was pounding and her legs felt so shaky that it was an effort to walk straight as she made for her desk. She sank onto her chair with a sigh of relief. 'Oh, does it feel good to sit down somewhere warm.'

'What do you mean?' Denise asked in concern.

'Oh, only that I got home last night looking—and feeling!—like a drowned rat to find that the water heater had packed up and that someone had cut through the power cables.' She tried to laugh but her throat rasped painfully. 'I spent the night huddled up in bed trying to keep warm!'

'No wonder you've caught a chill! But I really don't think you should be here, Karen. Apart from the fact that you obviously aren't well, there are the children to consider. Some of them are very susceptible to infections,' Denise declared worriedly.

Karen sighed, unable to argue against that. 'I suppose you're right. I wouldn't have come only I didn't feel quite so bad when I set off. I think it was the extra soaking I got waiting for a bus that didn't turn up which did the damage. I think I'd better take myself back home.'

She got up, then had to steady herself as the room started

to spin. Denise hurried to her side and eased her back into the chair.

'You're in no fit state to go anywhere like that!' she declared firmly. 'Stay there while I sort something out.'

Karen didn't have the strength to argue. Her head was swimming and making her feel sick. She closed her eyes, hoping that would improve things, but it didn't. A surge of nausea burnt her throat and she staggered to her feet. It was a relief when a firm hand took hold of her arm.

'Bathroom, from the look of you. Come on, sweetheart, move it!'

She raised dazed eyes but there was no time to question how Nick happened to be there as she felt bile rise into her throat again. She pressed a hand to her mouth and let him help her to the bathroom where she was violently and ingloriously sick. Frankly, she didn't think she could feel any worse at that point, but she was wrong. Discovering that Nick had followed her into the room and witnessed what had happened made her want to creep into a deep, dark hole and die!

'Come on, you'll probably feel a bit better now.'

His tone was as bracing as though he were addressing a small child and Karen succumbed to the urge to act accordingly. She could definitely feel a tantrum brewing, no doubt the result of her feeling both ill and mortified!

'I don't feel better, I feel rotten,' she declared mutinously, glaring at him.

'So I can see. Obviously not just an upset stomach, from the look of it.' He laid the back of his hand against her forehead. 'You're burning up too. How long have you been like this?'

'Does it matter?' she snapped back, hating the tingle of awareness which coursed through her body. For heaven's sake, he was playing *doctor* not trying to seduce her! she berated herself, but it didn't have much effect.

'Yes, it does. It matters a lot.' He folded his arms and continued to study her. It was obvious that he didn't intend to give in to her foul mood and Karen sighed as she realised how badly she was behaving.

'I think I caught a chill last night,' she muttered, avoiding his eyes. 'I got soaked on my way home from work. Then when I got there the water heater wouldn't work so I couldn't have a hot shower and there was no heating on because workmen had cut through the power cables.'

'Do you mean to say that you spent the night without any heating or lighting?' he demanded incredulously. 'Why didn't you phone me?'

She shrugged. 'What for?'

'Because I thought we were...friends, Karen.'

She shot him a wary glance, unsure whether she'd actually heard that hesitation in his voice. However, he wasn't looking at her as he reached for the phone and quickly punched in a number.

'Hugh, it's Nick. Is it OK with you if I take an hour off? I'll be back by...' he checked his watch '...ten-thirty at the latest. Great.'

He replaced the receiver, then looked round. 'Right, what do you need? Coat? Bag?'

He quickly scooped up the said articles, then took hold of her arm. 'That it, then? There's nothing else you need?'

'Need for what? Where are we going?' she demanded dazedly, wishing her head didn't feel as though it were going to spin right off her neck. She squinted at Nick, trying to keep him in focus, but he seemed to be jiggling around alarmingly.

'Home, of course. Denise called me and told me you

weren't well and she was right. You aren't in any fit state to be here, Karen.'

He steered her towards the door but she hung back, gripping hold of the desk to steady herself. 'But you don't need to take me,' she protested weakly. 'I can get a taxi or...or catch the bus.'

He laughed softly, yet there was a distinctly dangerous edge to the sound which it was hard to ignore. 'Can you, indeed? I don't think you could make it across this room on your own, quite frankly, let alone find your way home on a bus!'

His know-it-all attitude stung. Karen squared her shoulders and stared him in the eyes...or at least she tried to, because it was difficult to focus when he kept wobbling about. 'I am perfectly capable of looking after myself!'

To prove it she took a couple of steps away from the desk, but it was a mistake, she realised. Without its solid support, she saw the floor begin to rock up and down. It was rather like being on board a ship in the middle of a storm and she had never been a good sailor!

Nick got her to the bathroom just in time. He wiped her face with a wad of cool, damp paper towels, then dried it again with his own pristine white handkerchief. He didn't say a word while he was doing so but the expression on his face spoke volumes.

This time when he led her to the door Karen didn't utter a word of protest. She had learned her lesson the hard way yet again. When Nick left her sitting on a chair in the foyer while he went for his car, she didn't make any attempt to move until he came back for her.

'Right, take it nice and easy,' he said calmly, sliding his arm around her waist while he helped her to her feet. Karen felt weak tears gather behind her lids and blinked but they trickled down her face anyway. She felt so ill and the past few days had been so rotten that suddenly it was all too much for her.

'Come on, don't cry. You'll feel better soon,' he soothed, smiling into her tear-soaked eyes. 'Trust me: I'm a doctor!'

It wasn't really *that* funny but she couldn't help laughing at the trite expression. 'You really think that makes me feel better?' she demanded, sniffing noisily.

Nick produced the handkerchief again and gave it to her. 'No, but one can only hope for miracles, not perform them.'

He helped her to the car, making sure her seat belt was securely fastened before sliding behind the wheel. Karen rested her head against the soft leather upholstery as Nick put the car into gear. Maybe it was a combination of the cold and being sick all mixed up with the sleepless nights she'd had recently, but suddenly she felt too tired to keep her eyes open. She would just sit back and let Nick get her home safely...

'We're here. Wait there a moment while I unlock the door. There's no point you getting soaked again.'

Karen blinked as she was roused from her nap. She fumbled with her bag, trying to find her keys. Of course, sod's law dictated that they should be stuck right at the very bottom. 'I'll find them in a moment,' she muttered, digging through the jumble of *essential* items she carried with her each day. Lipstick, comb, three old bus tickets, half a packet of chewing gum and a withered apple all got churned around before she gave a triumphant cry.

Holding up the elusive keyring, she turned to Nick and discovered that the seat next to her was empty. She looked round in bemusement and only then realised that they weren't parked anywhere near where she lived. There certainly weren't *trees* in front of the old house where she had her flat, nor was there a lovely little *park* opposite. Where on earth were they? And why had Nick brought her here?

She barely had time to filter the questions through her mind before he opened the car door. His hand was firm as he took hold of her arm, his tone equally free of any shred of doubt. Obviously, *he* knew what was going on, but she didn't!

'Where are we?' she snapped, feeling too sick to temper the question with politeness. Nick didn't even blink.

'My house, of course. Come along, now. Let's get you inside.' He spoke with the same air of authority that he probably used when addressing a reluctant five-year-old. Karen heard it and resented it...bitterly!

'I am not going anywhere until you explain what is going on,' she declared, shooting a glance at the house they were parked in front of.

Her mind skittered off at a tangent as she realised what a gem of a place it was. One of a sweeping crescent all built of pale grey brick, with white painted windows and a shiny black door sporting an even shinier brass letter box, it looked like something out of an advert for good living. If she hadn't felt so ill and grouchy, then she would have been itching to go inside and have a good poke around, but right at that moment all she wanted was her own bed in her own tiny attic and nothing else!

'I've brought you to my house because at least you will be warm here,' Nick replied with a touch of asperity. 'Now, do you think we could continue this discussion inside if it's going to take more than thirty seconds? It may have escaped your notice, Karen, but it is absolutely pouring down and I'm getting soaked!'

'Oh!' She hadn't noticed and she flushed as she saw the wet patches on his jacket. Without another word she let him help her out of the car and into the house. He took her straight to a small sitting-room at the rear which overlooked a surprisingly large and lush garden. Urging her onto the sofa, he didn't even ask before swinging her legs up onto the cushions and covering them with a tartan rug.

'Just lie there while I lock the car and make you a drink,' he ordered, giving her no time to object before he left the room.

Karen took a small breath and ran a quick mental check-list of how she felt about being ordered around. Angry? No, that was too strong. Annoyed? Not really. Pleased? No way!

She sighed as she realised that it was impossible to gauge how she felt about the high-handed way Nick had behaved by bringing her here without prior consultation. It all depended on *why* he had done it, she supposed.

'Try this. It should help.'

Nick came back with a steaming glass of fragrant liquid in an elegant silver holder. He handed it to her, his brows drawing together as he watched her warily sniff it.

'It's honey and lemon, not poison,' he informed her tersely.

Karen took a sip, although she wasn't deaf to the harsh note in his voice. Nick sounded angry, but why? If anyone had the right to a grievance, then surely it was her?

'It's fine,' she announced, setting the glass on a coaster so that it wouldn't mark the little polished table he had placed conveniently close to the sofa.

'Good.' He strode across the room and picked up an armful of glossy magazines from a table by the window. He brought them back and placed them on the table next to the sofa. 'Something to read if you get bored, but my advice is to try and have a nap. It will do you more good.'

'I...I'll try,' Karen agreed quietly, more convinced than ever that something had upset him.

'I've phoned my cleaning lady and she will pop in around midday and make you a bit of lunch, if you feel like it,' he continued in the same clipped tone. 'The central heating is on but light the gas fire if you feel chilly; shall I show you how it works?'

'I'm sure I can figure it out. Thank you,' she whispered, feeling more and more hurt by his attitude.

'Fine. I'll leave you to it, then. As I say, just try to rest and I'm sure you'll feel better by this evening. I'll check with the electricity company to see when your power should be back on. Hopefully, you will be able to go home this evening.'

He swung round but Karen couldn't bear to let him leave like this. If he was angry with her, then she wanted to know why. 'Nick, what's wrong?'

He barely slowed as he opened the sitting-room door. 'Nothing. I'll see you later...'

'Of course there's something wrong!' she declared, swinging her feet to the floor, although she thought better of actually trying to stand as the room swam. She took a steadying breath and forced the tables and chairs to stop whirling around. However, her voice was more than a little quavery when she continued—less assertive than pleading, in fact.

'I know something has upset you but I don't know what. Is it something I've done?'

He took a deep breath and stared at the floor rather than looking at her. 'Yes and no. I suppose it just hurts to have it hammered home that you don't trust me, Karen.'

'Don't trust you,' she repeated blankly, her mouth a little agape as she stared at him. She snapped it shut, then licked her lips because they felt so dry all of a sudden. 'Wh-why do you think that, Nick?'

'Isn't it obvious?' He gave a bitter laugh as he turned to

face her and she was stunned by the depth of pain in his eyes. 'Your face was a picture when you realised I'd brought you here instead of taking you home. It never crossed your mind that the reason I had done so was because I couldn't bear the thought of you being in that flat with no heating when you're ill. You didn't *trust* me enough to know that I only have your best interests at heart, Karen. And that's what hurts!'

She didn't know what to say. The pain in his voice was so real that it had shocked her into silence. Nick gave her a grim smile, then left the room and a few seconds later she heard the front door closing. She half rose to her feet, then sank back onto the sofa. She wanted to call him back and tell him he was wrong, but maybe she needed to be certain that she was telling him the truth.

It was all a question of trust, that was what it came down to. And trusting anyone completely was the most difficult thing of all to do.

It was a funny sort of day, unlike any day she had lived through before. Karen lay on the sofa for most of the morning just letting her mind drift where it chose. She napped a couple of times and each time felt that bit better when she woke up. However, she stayed where she was and followed Nick's instructions to the letter. Frankly, it was the least she could do in the circumstances!

Nick's daily, Mrs Rogers, came in as promised and made her an omelette for her lunch with a small fresh-fruit salad for dessert. She was a motherly sort of woman and happily fussed around Karen, chattering on about her grandchildren and other snippets about her life.

It was all very soothing and Karen enjoyed the cosseting. After Mrs Rogers left, Karen went to the downstairs cloakroom and washed her hands, then brushed her hair. She grimaced as she took stock of her reflection in the mirror above the basin. Her cheeks were a lot more flushed than usual and her eyes looked overly bright, proof that although she might be feeling better she still hadn't shaken off the chill.

She decided to be the model patient and try to nap for an hour or so. Then when Nick got home she would ask him to drive her home whether or not the power had been restored. He had been kind enough to offer her his house for the day and she really couldn't impose on him any longer.

She went back to the sitting-room and curled up on the sofa again. Mrs Rogers had turned on the gas fire and the room was deliciously warm. Karen fell asleep in no time and only woke up when the front door slammed. She shot a surprised look at her watch and was stunned to find that it was five o'clock and that she had slept away the whole afternoon.

'Well, I'm glad to see that you've followed doctor's orders. I wish I had more patients like you!'

Nick came into the room, smiling as he saw her sleep-flushed face. Karen ran a smoothing hand over her hair, feeling more than a little disconcerted.

'I only meant to take a nap,' she explained ruefully, swinging her legs to the floor. 'But I went out like a light!'

'Then you must have needed the sleep.' Nick smiled at her again. He seemed back to his usual good-humoured self and Karen felt the small knot of anxiety she hadn't really been aware of until then melt away. She didn't want to fall out with Nick, she acknowledged. It hurt too much to know that they were at odds.

'I must have done. Anyway, I feel a lot better than I did this morning, I'm pleased to say.' She gathered up the rug.

'I really appreciate you letting me stay here today, Nick. Thank you.'

'It was my pleasure.' He shrugged lightly. 'I wouldn't have had a moment's peace worrying about you alone in that cold flat. Now, how about a drink? Think you can manage a glass of wine or would you prefer fruit juice?'

Karen hesitated. She didn't want Nick thinking that he had to entertain her when he must be tired after the busy day he'd had. 'Are you sure I won't be in the way?'

His brows rose. 'In the way of what, precisely? The only thing I am planning on doing is having a drink and something to eat.'

His tone softened, became so persuasive that Karen felt a frisson run under her skin. 'Can't you find it in your heart to take pity on a poor, lonely doctor who is badly in need of some company after a hard day at work?'

'Well...' She hadn't meant to weaken but it was hard to resist that beseeching note in his voice. Nick grinned as he saw from her face that he had got what he'd wanted.

'Great! So what's it to be, sweetheart? Wine or fruit juice?'

Her toes tingled as he used that endearment again. Karen shuffled her feet, trying to ignore the curling sensation spreading up her body. 'Juice, I think. Mrs Rogers gave me some paracetamol before so I'd prefer to steer clear of alcohol.'

'Mmm, good idea. Anyway, come into the kitchen and see what you want. I honestly can't remember what's in the fridge apart from orange juice and some disgusting concoction that Jamie adores!'

Karen laughed, although she couldn't help wondering how much time his nephew spent with him. Did Nick have Jamie here on his own? Or did Melanie stay as well?

The thought put a bit of a damper on her mood but she

tried not to dwell on it because it wouldn't do any good. She followed Nick into the kitchen and looked round appreciatively, taking stock of the sunny yellow walls and dark oak cabinets, the black-and-white tiled floor. There was even an Aga to cook on, its bright red paintwork adding another spot of cheerful colour to the room.

'This is a lovely kitchen,' she declared as Nick opened the fridge.

'I like it too,' he replied, grinning at her over the top of the open fridge door. 'My parents used to have a place in Surrey when we were kids and I always loved the kitchen there because it was where we spent so much of our time. I wanted to recreate that sort of feel when I bought this place. Ideally, I'd love to live in the country, you see, but it just isn't practical with my job. This is the next best option.'

'Your own rural idyll in the heart of the city,' Karen pronounced with a smile. She walked to the window and laughed as she looked out into the garden. 'I see it's even extended to the outdoors as well. Surely that can't be a tree-house out there? I must be seeing things!'

'You're not. Every male between the ages of one and one hundred needs a tree-house. It's a well-known fact.'

Karen couldn't help laughing. 'Well, it wasn't one I knew until now!' She peered through the glass, trying to make out the details better, but night had drawn in, making it hard to see clearly.

'I wish I could see it better,' she said a shade wistfully.

'Then your wish shall be granted, my lady.' Nick slammed the fridge door, then lifted an old waxed jacket off the peg behind the kitchen door and held it out for her. 'Put this on first because I don't want you catching more cold.'

Karen did as she was told, sliding her arms into the

jacket and zipping it up. Nick nodded approvingly as he opened the back door.

'You should be warm enough in that even though it's seen more years of use than I care to mention.'

He headed out into the garden, then paused to offer Karen his hand. 'Mind the step. We don't want you twisting your ankle.'

Karen shivered as she felt the warmth of his hand enclosing hers. The night was cool, the scent of the damp earth assailing her nostrils all the more sharply after her being indoors all day. She drew in a few deep lungfuls as Nick led her to the base of the tree. He paused to look up, squinting as he studied the rope-ladder which hung from one of the thick boughs on which the tree-house had been built.

'How good are you with heights?' he asked, glancing at her. 'It isn't that far up but it can seem like a long way if you aren't used to it.'

'Heights don't bother me,' she assured him quickly.

'Right, then, I'll go first so that I can give you a helping hand when you reach the top. If you feel at all nervous, though, just say so, Karen.' He suddenly laughed, his teeth gleaming whitely in the dusk. 'I'm not sure this is what a doctor should order for a patient who has been sick best part of the day!'

'Rubbish! I feel fine now. And I want to go up there and see what it's like.'

She smiled back at him, her heart turning over as he suddenly bent and dropped a kiss on the tip of her nose.

'Well, if that's what you want, then so be it!' he declared, laughing at her.

Karen took another lungful of spicy air as he began climbing the ladder. However, it did little to steady her racing heart. One kiss and it was tapping out a message she mustn't listen to. Nick was just being kind, treating her as he would treat any friend, she told herself. But it was hard to believe it when she didn't want to.

'OK, come on up.'

He had reached the platform and crouched down to call her up to him. Karen put her left foot firmly on the ladder and began her ascent. It took only a few seconds to reach the platform and Nick was there to help her, his hand reassuringly firm as it fastened around her wrist.

'Well done! You did that like a pro! Are you sure that you didn't have a tree-house of your own when you were a kid and you've been holding out on me?' he teased, drawing her away from the edge of the platform and into the small wooden cabin.

'Unfortunately not. Although I *always* wanted one!' she declared, standing still while he lit the gas lantern. She gasped in amazement as he held it aloft. 'It's fantastic! Don't tell me you made all this yourself?'

'Uh-huh.' There was satisfaction written all over Nick's face as he looked at the wooden table and chairs, the shelves which held a selection of toys and games. There was even something which looked like it could be a bed—sort of like a Japanese futon—covered in a thick patchwork quilt. Karen was amazed and didn't try to hide it from him.

'It's just wonderful. I don't know what to say!'

'I'm glad you like it.' Nick smiled at her, his face very gentle in the glow from the oil lamp. 'I wanted it to be special, a place where Jamie could come and play and feel like he was in control. All too often a child with a disability like his lacks independence. But here he can do what he wants to—play out his games and be perfectly safe.'

Karen felt her eyes mist with tears. That Nick should have gone to so much trouble for his nephew touched her deeply. It just went to prove once again what a kind man he was.

'He must love it here,' she said softly, looking around so that he wouldn't see how moved she was.

'He does. He spends every spare minute he gets up in this tree-house when he stays with me.' Nick paused to looked around and his voice was filled with sadness as he added softly, 'Ed and I had a tree-house just like it when we were children. I modelled it on that.'

'Your brother would have been so pleased to know how much you've done for his son,' Karen said quietly. 'You love Jamie such a lot that it must help make up for the fact that his father is dead.'

Nick sighed sadly. 'I hope so, but my input can never match what a real father's would be. Still, maybe that will all be resolved in the near future. Anyway, come on out to the deck; you can see for miles on a clear night.'

Karen followed him outside although her heart felt like a lead weight. Had that been an allusion to the fact that he and Melanie were making plans for their future together? she wondered.

It was hard to tell and she didn't have the courage to ask him outright because she was afraid what the answer might be. She didn't say anything as she went to the far side of the platform, but the view which met her was so marvellous that it was impossible to remain silent.

'It's incredible!' she declared, staring into the distance.

'Isn't it just? You should see it on a summer evening. I spend ages up here just enjoying the view.'

'I can understand why,' Karen declared, fascinated by the lights of the city shimmering below them.

'Look, there's St Paul's Cathedral. You can see the dome.'

Nick turned her so that she could see where he was pointing to, his hands resting lightly on her shoulders. Karen shivered as she felt the warmth of his hands flowing through the thickness of her jacket. The night was cold yet the warmth from his hands seemed to be sending waves of heat through her veins.

'Are you cold?' Nick asked in concern, feeling the tremor which passed through her.

'No...I mean, yes...' She stumbled over her answer and saw his eyes darken as they searched her face.

'Was that a yes or a no, Karen?' he asked in a silky-smooth tone which only made her shiver all the harder. She stared at him in confusion and saw his mouth curl into a smile which held a wealth of emotions.

'Or maybe it's both?' he suggested softly, bending towards her. His lips found hers, gently, delicately, yet deliberately seeking to tease an answer out of her. Karen knew that he had got the one he wanted as her lips parted of their own accord. She seemed powerless to control them, unable to make them behave and do what she wanted them to.

His mouth became more urgent as he felt her respond, the kiss more demanding, yet it was still steeped in that tenderness which was such an integral part of him. Karen realised then that she couldn't have resisted even if she'd wanted to.

She kissed him back without reservation then, her lips clinging to his, her arms twining around his neck as tightly as his fastened around her. She could feel the heavy beat of his heart beneath her breast, the pressure of his body against the softness of hers, and her heart went wild as she realised that Nick was as stirred by the kiss as she was.

When he unzipped her jacket so that he could reach her breasts she moaned, shocked by her own instantaneous response to the caressing touch of his fingers. It felt like flying without a safety net! Her senses lifting to the heavens and soaring above them, wild and free.

Nick was breathing hard when they broke apart, but then so was she. No one could have remained immune to the soul-stirring beauty of that kiss. His eyes were heavy with passion as they traced her face, glittering with a hunger he didn't try to hide.

'I didn't get you up here to seduce you, Karen, but that's what is going to happen if we don't stop this now.'

Karen heard the harsh grate of his voice and struggled to get herself together. It didn't quite work. 'Is it?'

She winced at the inanity of the question but Nick just laughed as though he understood the difficulty she was having thinking straight. 'Uh-huh. No doubt about it.'

He dropped another kiss on her mouth, then drew back with evident reluctance. 'But it wouldn't be right, would it?'

Why not? she wanted to ask before the answer hit her like a dash of cold water. Because it wouldn't be right to seduce one woman while he was in love with another! Nick had too many principles to allow himself to get carried away by the mood and the moment. He would never treat a woman the way Paul had treated her, as a brief amusement, a way to sate his urges. Oh, he might have been tempted; he was honest enough to admit that. But he would never betray Melanie's trust that way!

Afterwards, Karen wasn't sure where she found the strength to answer calmly when it felt as though she had been dealt the bitterest blow of her life. Now there was no way she could avoid the truth any longer, no way that she could escape the simple fact that Nick was in love with his sister-in-law. It was just the thought of how embarrassed he would be if she broke down which helped her get through the moment.

'You're right,' she said quietly, every scrap of emotion held in check. 'It would be silly to do something we would only regret at the end of the day.'

'I...I think so too.'

Oddly enough, his voice sounded far more strained than it had done. Karen shot him a wary glance, but he had already made his way to the ladder. He glanced back and his face gave nothing away.

'I'll go first, shall I? Just take your time and don't try to rush.'

Karen nodded, waiting until he had disappeared over the side of the platform before she turned to take a last look at the view. The sky was velvety black now that the rain-clouds had blown away, a few early stars twinkling like diamonds too bright for even the reflection from the street lights to dim their brilliance.

She closed her eyes and committed the scene to memory—not that there was much chance of her forgetting it. For a few brief minutes she had been touched by magic before reality had intruded once more. Now she had to get on with being who and what she was, and she wasn't the woman Nick was in love with. How that thought hurt!

CHAPTER TEN

'I'M SO glad that you're pleased, Mrs Harper-Ward. And I really appreciate you phoning to let me know.'

Karen paused as the woman on the other end of the phone broke into more effusive thanks. She felt a little guilty that Helena's recent progress wasn't really down to her. Francesca, the child's nanny, should really take the credit for it. However, there was little she could do without breaking the Italian girl's confidence and that was something she wanted to avoid.

She cut in smartly when the other woman paused to draw breath. 'My suggestion is that Helena keeps her next appointment and then I shall review her case. I think that would be the best idea, don't you?'

Another effusive round of thanks ensued before Karen was able to hang up. She sighed as she saw Denise looking at her questioningly. 'Helena Harper-Ward's mother.'

'She isn't still worried about her daughter, surely?' Denise queried.

'Oh, no. She's delighted with Helena's progress and that's why she rang...to thank me,' Karen explained swiftly.

'Good. Then why are you so down in the dumps?' Denise shrugged when Karen looked at her in surprise. 'You've seemed very subdued since you were off sick, in fact. I put it down to the fact that you were still a bit under the weather, but maybe that isn't it. Tell me to mind my own business if you want to, but have you and Nick fallen out?'

Karen shook her head, although it was impossible to deny what Denise had said. She had tried her best not to let what had happened affect her working life, but being thrust into daily contact with Nick wasn't easy. Oh, he'd been his usual pleasant, considerate self, but Karen was so afraid of making a fool of herself that she was constantly on her guard.

She knew that Nick was puzzled by her behaviour, but each time he'd tried to talk to her she had made up some excuse. Whenever he had asked her out after work—for a drink or a visit to the cinema—she had claimed that she was too busy. He hadn't asked her for three or four days now so she was fairly confident that he had got the message, although several times she had noticed him watching her with concern.

She cut short that thought, knowing how foolish it was to dwell on it. It was clutching at straws to read anything into how he looked at her. If Nick was concerned, then it was purely because he cared for her as a friend.

'Not at all. Nick and I are just friends. There isn't anything going on between us.'

'No?' Denise sounded surprised. 'I got the impression that he—' She suddenly stopped. 'Sorry. It isn't any of my business, is it? It's just that playing "mum" tends to become a habit so that you end up poking your nose into everyone's affairs!'

Karen laughed at that. 'You aren't poking your nose into anything, Denise! And I'm sorry if I haven't been up to par lately. Perhaps it is the after-effects of that chill.'

'More than likely. You did well to shrug it off as fast as you did. Some of these bugs seem to hit like lightning then disappear almost overnight. Look at young Jamie. Hugh was only saying how relieved he was that it hadn't been the implant causing Jamie all those problems, but strep throat. Poor Hugh must have aged ten years worrying about it, but it's understandable in the circumstances.'

'What do you mean?' Karen queried.

'Because of Melanie, of course.' Denise frowned when she saw Karen's bewilderment. 'Hugh's crazy about her; didn't you know?'

'I had no idea. And how…how does she feel about him?' Karen asked weakly, her heart lodged in her throat as she waited for the answer. Had she got it wrong and misread the situation? However, Denise just sighed as she went to the door.

'I've no idea. Neither has poor Hugh, which makes it all the more difficult for him, I imagine. Right, I'd better make a start. Am I right in thinking that Kevin is coming in today?'

'You are.' Karen was still trying to absorb what she had learned, but she forced herself to concentrate. 'He's coming after school. One of his teachers is giving him a lift here and Ian's parents have offered to run him home later on.'

'I must say that it's worked out wonderfully well. Both those boys are benefiting from the visits and Ian's parents are thrilled that he has something to look forward to,' Denise declared.

'I know. I was talking to his mother a few days ago and she told me how glad she was that Ian had found a friend.' Karen sighed sadly. 'Evidently, Ian's tumour is inoperable so all they can do is keep him comfortable and happy.'

'Does he know?' Denise asked with a catch in her voice. She smiled sadly at Karen. 'When you have a son of your own it brings it home to you all the more.'

'It must do,' she assured her. 'And, yes, Ian knows. His parents decided that he should be told and evidently he has accepted the idea, even explained to Kevin that he won't be around much longer. That's why Kevin asked if he could

come to see him more often. Apparently, Kevin spends
every spare moment bird-watching so that he can tell Ian
what he has seen.'

'Kevin's a real gutsy little boy. He deserves better than
the parents he's got. Still, isn't it great to know that you've
achieved so much, Karen? It makes all our hard work worth
while.'

Denise left after that and Karen smiled as she went back
to the notes she was preparing. It *was* a good feeling to
know that she had helped the children. It was the reason
why she had gone into the profession. It also helped to
offset the pain which seemed to be her constant companion
lately, although Denise's revelations about Hugh
Derbyshire made her put down her pen as she thought about
them. She had never suspected that the consultant was in
love with Melanie yet, now that she thought about it, she
remembered how attentive he had been to Melanie at that
party.

She sighed as she picked up her pen again. She *was*
clutching at straws this time! Maybe Hugh *did* care for
Melanie, but that didn't necessarily mean she reciprocated
his feelings, did it? There was no guarantee that love given
would be returned.

That thought caused her yet more pain, although once
again she refused to examine it too closely. Karen knew
that she was deliberately avoiding the issue of why the
thought of Nick and his sister-in-law being in love hurt her
so much, but she was afraid to face up to it. If she didn't
admit the reason to herself, then maybe it wouldn't hurt so
much.

The morning passed quickly as usual. Karen had a new
referral to see that day, a boy named Andrew Gunner.
Andrew was seven years old and had been referred by the
community nurse after she had noticed that there appeared

to be a problem with his speech when she had visited his school.

Apparently, Andrew's parents were both partially deaf and neither had detected the problem themselves, nor had his teachers picked up on it as he was a very quiet boy and never said much in class. He'd been referred for hearing tests initially but there was no problem in that area. Karen had been asked to make her own assessment and it soon became apparent that there was indeed a problem.

Andrew's speech had a very nasal quality, reminiscent of someone with a cleft palate. However, after examining his mouth, Karen could see no evidence of anything wrong. She was so puzzled that she decided that she wanted to get to the root of the child's problem there and then.

She phoned through to the ENT clinic and as luck would have it there had been a cancellation so she was able to take Andrew there to be seen straight away. His parents accompanied her and were obviously worried even though she did her best to reassure them. Leaving them in the waiting area, she went to speak to Lorraine Cummings, the nurse on duty that day.

'Hi, I've brought Andrew Gunner with me. I just phoned and you said that someone would see him straight away,' she explained.

'That's right. You're in luck as Nick has a free half-hour, which is a rare thing indeed in this department!' Lorraine told her cheerfully, leading the way to the consulting-room to knock on the door. A deep voice called out that they could go in and Karen steeled herself. If she'd known that Nick would be the one to see the child then she would never have asked for an appointment, she thought, then realised how silly that would have been. She couldn't allow personal feelings to get in the way of her work!

'Thanks for fitting me in, Nick,' she said brightly as

Lorraine closed the door. 'I need some help to solve this little puzzle.'

'That's OK.' Nick said easily, but there was a definite restraint about his manner which hurt even though she knew it was silly. She couldn't expect a warm reception when she had acted so distantly towards him recently.

'Hello, Andrew. My name is Nick Bentley and I'm an ear, nose and throat doctor.' He introduced himself to the boy, then glanced at Karen again. 'Are his parents not with him?'

'Yes, but they preferred to wait outside. Mr and Mrs Gunner are both deaf, you see, and they decided it would be easier if I brought Andrew in to see you and then relayed what you'd said to them afterwards,' she explained. 'Oh, and for the record, Andrew's hearing isn't a problem, nor do I think it's the fact that his parents' speech isn't as clear as it would be normally. He sounds very nasal to me, almost like I would expect a child with a cleft palate to sound.'

'I understand.' Nick smiled more warmly this time. 'Right, I'll take a look and then you can report back to his mum and dad. Obviously, they trust you to look after him and who can blame them?'

He turned to the child, sitting Andrew down in a chair and positioning a lamp so that he could examine the boy's mouth and throat. Karen took a small breath but her heart was knocking against her ribcage because the compliment had had its usual devastating effect!

She waited in silence while Nick made his examination. He switched off the lamp at last and ruffled the boy's hair. 'Well done. You were really patient putting up with me poking around!'

Andrew smiled happily. When Nick asked him if he would go and wait with his parents he readily agreed.

'Nice kid,' Nick observed thoughtfully. 'Seems very well adjusted, too.'

'He is. You should see him signing to his parents. He puts me to shame!'

'Nonsense! The fact that you bothered to learn how to sign in the first place is to your credit, Karen.' Nick treated her to the warmest of warm smiles which made her knees go weak. She held onto the edge of the desk, afraid that she would keel over. Had he any idea what he did to her equilibrium every time he smiled at her like that? She hoped not!

'Sorry. What was that?' She suddenly realised that she had missed what he'd said.

'Just that it's a very rare condition and I can't be one hundred per cent certain that I'm right until he's had an X-ray. I've only seen one other case of submucous cleft since I started here.'

Karen frowned. 'I recall reading something about it in a journal once. Isn't it a cleft in the palate which has been covered over by the mucous membrane that lines the mouth?'

'That's it exactly. As you know, most clefts are apparent from the moment a child is born, but this can go undetected for some time. Usually, it's the parents who realise that their child sounds odd when he or she starts to speak.' Nick shrugged. 'However, in Andrew's case, obviously his parents were unable to detect the abnormality which is why it hasn't been picked up before now.'

'So what happens now?' Karen asked worriedly. 'You can do something for him, I hope? It isn't too late?'

'Oh, yes. There's no problem about that. We'll operate to close the palate and that will sort things out like magic.'

'Wonderful!' Karen declared, smiling at him. She felt her smile fade as she saw the way he was looking at her, with a kind of hungry urgency she didn't understand. Why should he look at *her* like that when it was Melanie he wanted?

'Right, we'd better go and explain it all to his parents, hadn't we?'

Nick was all business once more as he led the way from the room. Karen followed him out to waiting area but she left it up to him to explain to Andrew's parents what would happen next. Frankly, she doubted she would have been much help at that moment when her mind felt in such turmoil. Nick kept giving out such mixed signals that she didn't know if she was coming or going! One day she was sure he was in love with his sister-in-law and the next...

Her heart began to drum. Could it be that Nick felt something for *her* after all? And wasn't it about time that she tried to find out?

'Mind if I sit here?'

Karen looked up as Nick stopped by her table. It was lunch-time and she had decided to go to the canteen that day although she had avoided it for the past week so she wouldn't run into Nick. However, she had made up her mind that there was no way she could keep putting off the moment of truth any longer. She *had* to know how he felt about Melanie, although she was suddenly beset with doubts when she saw him standing there.

Was it really wise to bring matters to a head when she wasn't sure what the outcome would be?

'It's busy in here today, isn't it?' Nick observed as he pulled out a chair.

'Yes, it is,' she concurred, steadfastly ignoring the dozen or more empty tables. She flushed as she saw Nick's mouth quirk because they both knew it was a lie. Obviously, he was as keen to speak to her as she'd been to speak to him and she didn't know whether to feel glad or sorry.

Picking up her fork, she pushed her salad around her plate as he set about unloading his tray. Her nerves were knotted with impatience, but if he was aware of the tension he gave little sign as he lined up his cutlery with regimental precision. It was only when he dropped his teaspoon onto the floor that Karen realised how nervous he was. It was such a contradiction in terms—Nick Bentley being *nervous*—that she gaped at him in surprise.

He gave a rueful shake of his head as he tossed the offending spoon onto the tray. 'So much for the cool, calm, collected approach. I haven't felt this screwed up since I was sixteen!'

'Wh-why?' she stammered.

'Because I desperately want to sort out what is happening between us, Karen.' He shrugged but she could see the pain in his eyes. 'You've been avoiding me ever since that night we went up into the tree-house together and I need to know why. If I've done something to upset you, then won't you tell what it is?'

'You...you haven't upset me, Nick.' She tried to laugh but the sound came out all wrong. Now that the moment had arrived she was suddenly scared. How could she come out and ask him how he felt about Melanie? Wouldn't he want to know *why* she was interested and then what would she say? She wasn't sure that she was ready to admit her reasons even to herself just yet.

She avoided his eyes as she stared at her plate. 'I've been very busy lately.'

'So busy that you've given up eating lunch? So busy that you haven't had time to come for a drink with me after work?' His tone was sceptical. 'What exactly have you been doing that's kept you so busy that you haven't had even an hour to spare, Karen?'

'Oh, this and that.' She shrugged, wishing with her whole heart that she hadn't started this because she wasn't ready to face the repercussions it could cause. 'Y-you know how it is when you're in work all day; there's always something which needs doing, isn't there?'

'That's what I've been telling myself, but I don't really believe it.' His tone was harsh all of a sudden and she looked at him in surprise, feeling her heart lurch as she saw the anger in his eyes.

'Come on, Karen, why not tell me the truth? You don't want to see me because you've met someone else, haven't you? That's why you've turned down all my invitations lately.' He laughed contemptuously. 'I just don't understand why you're making such a big deal of it.'

It was obvious that *he* didn't consider it to be very important! Karen felt her blood turn to ice as she heard the dismissive note in his voice. It was patently obvious that Nick couldn't have cared less if she *had* been seeing somebody else!

The thought stung unbearably yet she refused to let him guess how much it had hurt. 'I wasn't making a *big deal* of it. I just didn't realise that I was accountable for my actions to you or anyone else, for that matter!'

His eyes seemed to bore right through her. 'I never said that you were. I just thought that we were friends, Karen. And in my book friends tell each other the truth instead of making up excuses!' He pushed back his chair. 'Anyway, don't worry about it. Now that I know the score, I won't be making any more claims on your time. Enjoy your lunch.'

He left the canteen, leaving his lunch untouched on the table. Karen waited until she was sure he would have gone before she went back to her office. She sat at her desk going over and over everything that had been said, wishing that she had handled things better. Yet what difference would it have made? Nick had made it plain how he felt about her, that she was a friend and nothing more than that. Oh, perhaps he had been annoyed at the thought of her *lying* to him, but that was understandable. The idea that she might be involved with another man certainly hadn't bothered him!

At the end of the day she had achieved her objective and found out how he felt. The situation certainly wouldn't have been improved if she had come out and told him that she was in love with him!

The thought slipped in before she could stop it. Karen felt a great cloud of sadness envelop her. She wanted to tell herself that it wasn't true but she knew in her heart that she couldn't lie any longer. She was in love with Nick Bentley. It was the last thing she had wanted to happen but she couldn't change it!

'I th-th-think it's a kestrel!'

It was a little after four o'clock and Karen was taking Kevin Walters up to see Ian. It had been difficult to concentrate all afternoon but she forced herself to respond as she heard the boy's excitement. It wasn't fair to take her unhappiness out on Kevin.

'And you saw it close to the hospital, did you?' she asked, thinking how much more animated Kevin looked than the first time she had met him. Whether it was the visits to Ian or the fact that Ian's parents made such a fuss of him, she wasn't sure. Probably a combination of both, she decided as the lift stopped. Everyone needed to feel loved and wanted.

'Yes. It was-s-s-s flying near those t-t-trees at the front.'

Kevin got out of the lift and started hurrying along the corridor to his friend's room. 'I must tell Ian!'

Karen followed him and said hello to Ian before she went to have a word with Lisa Fletcher, the sister on duty that day.

'Ian's been looking forward to Kevin's visit,' she told Karen. 'He hasn't been too good today but he perked up as soon as I reminded him that Kevin would be in to see him this afternoon.'

'I take it that his condition hasn't improved?' Karen asked sadly.

'I'm afraid not.' Lisa sighed. 'It's a case of making sure he's pain-free and gets as much pleasure as possible out of every day. Frankly, Kevin's visits are the highlight of his week.'

There wasn't much either of them could add to that. Karen returned to her office thinking how cruel life could be at times. She couldn't imagine what Ian's parents must be going through at this difficult time. It helped put her own feelings into perspective, although the pain wouldn't go away. Realising that she was in love with Nick, and how futile it was, wasn't something she would get over in a hurry.

She sorted out some paperwork then went to find Denise to check what needed doing for the next group session planned for the following day. As it would involve an older age group than the last one, she wanted to be sure that she was prepared.

They ran through various points they needed to cover and then it was time to collect Kevin. Karen had just stepped out of the lift when she heard a commotion at the far end of the corridor. She went to see what was happening and found a group of people in the day-room, peering anxiously out of the window.

'What's going on?' she asked, going over to Lisa Fletcher.

'It's Kevin.' Lisa's face was full of concern as she pointed to the fire-escape which was just visible from where they stood. 'I heard the emergency exit door being opened and came to see what was going on. Kevin's gone out onto the fire-escape to help a bird which seems to have got itself trapped.'

'No!' Karen exclaimed in horror, staring out of the window as well. She could see Kevin on the fire-escape, struggling to disentangle a bird which had become trapped in the netting which was used to keep pigeons off the building.

'Have you told him to come in?' she asked anxiously.

'Yes, but he won't answer. I've sent for Security but I'm scared that he'll be so frightened by the sight of some stranger coming after him that he might slip,' Lisa explained worriedly.

'Maybe it would help if I tried to persuade him to come back inside,' Karen suggested immediately. 'He knows me so he shouldn't be frightened.'

'Good idea! Come on, let's give it a try.'

Lisa led the way to the emergency exit door and quickly explained to the staff who had gathered there what Karen wanted to do. She gave Karen an encouraging smile when everyone agreed it was a good idea. 'OK, it's up to you now. I don't envy you, though. I hate heights!'

'They don't bother me, thankfully.' Karen summoned a smile, hoping that she wasn't being overly confident. It had been one thing going up to that tree-house, but it was quite another to climb out onto a narrow metal staircase several storeys above the ground.

She stepped carefully onto the platform by the door, feeling the wind tugging at her legs as she began to ascend the steps. Kevin was midway between two floors and she willed him not to do anything silly.

'Kevin, it's me, Karen. I want you to come back inside now, there's a good boy.' she told him as she got closer.

'C-c-c-can't. Must set him free or he-e-e—he'll die!'

Kevin barely glanced at her as he carried on trying to free the bird. It had its talons caught in the mesh and Karen knew that it wouldn't be able to get free by itself. However, her main priority had to be Kevin's safety.

'I understand, Kevin. But I still want you to come back with me. I'll make sure the bird is set free. I promise you.'

The boy glanced uncertainly at her. 'You might be t-t-t-telling me that to g-g-get me back inside.'

Karen could understand why he found it so hard to believe that she wouldn't lie to him. In Kevin's world she doubted that promises ever meant anything. It was a question of trust and she knew how hard it could be putting one's trust in anyone.

'I give you my solemn promise that I shall set him free, Kevin,' she said softly, a lump coming to her throat as she realised how she had come to trust Nick and expect him to be there for her when she needed him. The thought of living out the rest of her days without him was almost more than she could bear.

'Cross your heart and hope to die,' Kevin demanded with no hint of a stammer.

'Yes. Only I'm too scared to let go of this ladder to cross my heart,' she declared, smiling at him although her heart felt as though it were breaking.

He stared at her for a moment, then slowly reached out and stroked the bird. 'You'll be all right. I won't let anyone hurt you,' he whispered to it.

It stared back at him with unblinking yellow eyes, seeming almost to understand what the boy had said. It certainly didn't struggle as Kevin began to back down the ladder.

Karen heaved a sigh of relief as she descended the ladder and stepped back onto terra firma. However, her relief was short-lived as she was suddenly confronted by Nick, but it was a Nick she barely recognised. She most definitely hadn't seen him looking so angry before!

'I could shake you for what you just did!' he bit out, his eyes blazing at her. He did just that, caught hold of her by her shoulders and shook her, then suddenly pulled her into his arms and held her as though he would never let her go.

'You silly little fool, you scared the life out of me just now!'

Karen heard the throbbing note in his voice and took a deep breath. It didn't do anything to help her make sense of what was happening. Why had Nick looked at her as though...as though the thought of anything happening to her was more than he could bear?

'I...erm...' She got no further as Kevin scrambled back inside just then. Nick let her go and turned to him. His voice was very stern but oddly the child didn't appear at all afraid.

'That was a very silly thing to do, young man. You could have been badly hurt if you'd slipped.'

Kevin just shrugged. He looked at Karen and she saw the pleading expression in his eyes. She knew then that if she let him down she would be betraying all the trust he had placed in her.

'I have to go back up there to set that bird free.' She turned to Nick, her eyes beseeching him to understand, but understand what? That she had made a promise and must keep it? Or that she loved him so much that it hurt? She wasn't sure what she was trying to tell him at that moment, but she knew from the indrawn breath he took that he understood.

He touched her cheek, lightly, then turned to the boy. 'Will you let me go instead of Karen? You see, I can't bear the thought of her putting herself at risk again.'

It wasn't what he'd said but the way he'd said it. Karen's heart swelled until she thought it would burst. She was barely aware of Kevin agreeing as Nick turned to her once more.

'I won't be long,' he assured her, staring into her eyes. 'Will you wait here for me, Karen?'

Yes! she wanted to scream. I'll wait for ever and then some! However, all she said was a demure little 'Yes' which earned her a wicked chuckle by way of reply.

It took Nick only a few minutes to cut through the netting with a knife one of the nurses fetched from the kitchen. The bird was freed at last and everyone clapped as it flew away, apparently unharmed by its adventure. Nick was given a hero's welcome as he came back inside, but he shrugged off the praise.

'Kevin is the hero here. Although I sincerely hope he won't pull another stunt like that in a hurry!'

Everyone laughed as they went back to work. Karen rested her hand on Kevin's shoulder as she looked at Nick. 'I'll just make sure that Kevin is all right. Ian's parents are going to drive him home.'

It was funny how suddenly she could concentrate on all the mundane and necessary things when she'd found it so hard to do so earlier. However, there was something particularly sweet about putting off the moment they both knew would come.

Nick smiled at her and his eyes said everything he couldn't with Kevin listening. 'You do that. I'll have a word with Martyn Lennard and let him know what's happened. There'll probably be a bit of an enquiry but at least there was no harm done. I'll meet you in the foyer and we can go back to my house. Is that all right?'

'Fine,' she assured him, leading Kevin out of the room before the temptation to linger got the better of her. She took a deep breath, then let it out slowly and with it went all the pain and heartache.

Suddenly, she felt as free as that bird must have felt. She loved Nick and he loved her. Oh, she had no proof, but she didn't need it. She was just going to trust her instincts for once!

CHAPTER ELEVEN

NICK met her in the foyer a short time later. By tacit consent neither of them mentioned what was uppermost on both their minds as they drove to his house. Maybe Nick felt the same as she did—that he didn't want to rush things so there would be no mistakes made.

Karen followed him inside the house and went straight to the sitting-room. She put her bag on the sofa, then turned to find Nick holding out his arms to her. She stepped into them and it felt as though she was coming home at last.

'I love you, Karen. I can't tell you how much I've longed to say that.'

His voice grated with emotion and she smiled. 'Try,' she whispered. 'I want to know it all—how long you've known that you love me, when you first realised how you felt—everything!'

'So that you can believe I'm telling you the truth?'

She sensed the underlying pain to the question and hurried to reassure him. 'No! I do believe you, Nick. Oh, I'm not saying that I won't *enjoy* having you convince me, but I do believe you.'

She reached up and brushed his mouth with a kiss. 'I know I can trust you not to lie to me about anything, you see.'

'Darling!' His mouth was as hungry as hers was so that the kiss turned into an explosion of passion all the more poignant because neither of them had believed it would happen at one point.

Karen's cheeks were wet with tears when Nick lifted his

head, but they were tears of joy she was crying, not sadness. 'I love you so much, Nick Bentley. I didn't mean to fall in love with you but somehow you managed to steal my heart!'

'Good!' He sounded so smug that she couldn't help laughing. Nick laughed with her as he hugged her tight.

'OK, I know how self-satisfied that sounded but give me a break. It's like having Christmas and my birthday all rolled into one and *then* winning the lottery on top to know that I've finally convinced you that I'm worthy of your love!'

'Was that how I made you feel?' she teased. 'Unworthy? The great Nick Bentley...'

She squealed as his arms tightened. The kiss was long and very thorough so that they were both out of breath when it ended.

'I hope you feel suitably punished for your cheek, young woman,' he growled menacingly.

Karen smiled. 'Well, I'm not sure. Maybe a hundred lines would be more effective. How about if I write out "I must not give cheek to the man I love"? Would that be better, do you think?'

'How about you give me a hundred *kisses* instead, then we can both enjoy it?' Nick retorted, reaching for her again.

He sighed as he reluctantly let her go. 'What you do to my equilibrium isn't worth mentioning, sweetheart. I feel as though I'm on one of those fairground roller coasters whenever I'm with you...sort of all churned up and confused.'

'But you know that you love me,' she reminded him pertly, marvelling at her own new-found confidence.

'That is the one thing I *do* know. I can even conjugate the verb. I love you. You love me. We love each other.'

He smiled at her with a world of tenderness in his eyes. 'Sounds great, doesn't it?'

'It does,' she agreed softly.

There was another satisfying interlude before Nick drew her to the sofa and pulled her down beside him. Settling her head in the crook of his shoulder, she sighed. 'I never thought it could feel like this.'

'Falling in love, you mean?' He kissed the top of her head, his lips stirring the soft red curls. 'Neither did I.'

'So you haven't been in love before?' she asked, wanting to know everything about him. She laughed as she realised how funny that was and felt rather than saw him frown.

'What's so amusing?' he demanded, tipping her face up so that he could look at her.

'Only that I can distinctly recall making up my mind to keep you at arm's length when we first met and here I am wanting to know all about you!'

'Mmm, I got the feeling that you had some sort of master plan. I think that was what piqued my interest, although it could have had something to do with the fact that you were so beautiful...and adorable...and sexy...'

He punctuated the words with kisses and Karen sighed dreamily when he stopped. 'Run out of adjectives, Dr Bentley?'

'Not at all. But I wouldn't like you getting *too* big-headed.' He kissed her quickly when she gasped, then grinned. 'Just teasing. In my view you are perfect the way you are, Karen.'

She heard the sincerity in his voice and flushed. 'Thank you. I feel pretty much the same...about you, I mean. I tried to find things about you to dislike but it was so hard!'

He chuckled as he drew her back into his arms. 'That's nice to know. At least you can't claim that you haven't tested out all my bad points. You won't have a leg to stand on after we're married if you try to change your mind.'

'Married!' She gulped in a breath, then rounded on him. 'But I haven't... You haven't...We...'

'No, we haven't, have we? We haven't discussed it because we haven't got that far.' He cupped her face between his hands and looked into her eyes. 'I'm going too far too fast, aren't I? And that's something I swore I wouldn't do.'

'Did you?' she asked, distracted by the way he was looking at her. Had any woman ever been looked at in such a way before? she wondered, seeing the fire which burned in his eyes, the wealth of tenderness and love.

'Yes. I knew how scared you were, Karen, and how difficult you found it to trust anyone.' His voice roughened. 'No wonder after the experience you had with that Paul guy. If I could have got my hands on him after you told me what he had done I would have cheerfully torn him limb from limb.'

She pressed her fingers against his mouth. 'Don't! It's all over and done with now. Paul is part of my past and I don't intend to let him ruin my future. I love you, Nick. And I know now that what I felt for Paul certainly wasn't love.'

'Thank heavens for that!' He rested his forehead against hers and his voice was thick with emotion. 'I was so afraid that I wouldn't be able to match up to that guy.'

'There's no question of you matching up to him! You are way above Paul in every respect. Frankly, I can't imagine what I even saw in him now, let alone why I was so heartbroken about what he did.'

'Having your trust betrayed like that isn't easy to come to terms with, Karen, so you mustn't blame yourself.' He kissed her tenderly. 'I just hope that you realise that you are safe with me because I swear on my life that I shall never, ever betray your trust.'

'I do know that, Nick.' Her voice broke and she gave him a wobbly smile. 'I love you *and* trust you completely.'

She sniffed noisily, then looked at him. 'So when did you realise that you were in love with me?'

'Are you sure this can't wait until later?' he murmured, drawing her closer.

'You were the one who said that you didn't want to go too fast,' she reminded him primly, although her pulse was racing at the expression in his eyes.

'Me and my big mouth! You have my permission to tell me to shut up the next time I get my priorities mixed up.' He sighed as he settled her against his side once more. 'But you're right. I don't want there to be any more mistakes between us, sweetheart.'

'You called me that at your father's birthday party,' she said dreamily. 'I can remember how it made me feel too.'

'If it was anything like the way I felt that night, then I sympathise!' He laughed as she gasped. 'I think it was when I kissed you when the lights went out that I realised just how I felt about you. Up till then I'd been trying to convince myself that I was just attracted to you and that it was understandable because you were so beautiful.

'I can remember looking at you one day in the canteen and getting this funny feeling that I'd reached a turning point in my life but I tried to ignore it. It was impossible, though. I was already well and truly under your spell by then.'

'Thank you. You can tell me things like that any day of the week,' she teased, although her heart had skipped a beat at the confession.

'Oh, don't worry, I shall!' Nick dropped a kiss on her nose, then sighed. 'When you told me about Paul, however,

I knew just how difficult it was going to be convincing you of how I felt. I'd always sensed that you were wary of me and had worked out that it probably had something to do with a relationship which had gone wrong. Finding out just how wrong things had gone for you scared me stiff.'

'In case I wasn't ever able to trust anyone again?' She smiled wistfully. 'I thought I wouldn't ever be able to, Nick. I was so afraid of getting hurt. Yet I found myself becoming more and more attracted to you. It was so hard to know what to do and then there was the question of Melanie, which just helped confuse things even more.'

'What do you mean?' His brows pleated as he stared at her. Karen smoothed the lines away with the tip of her finger, smiling as she felt him shudder. It was hard to think straight when he looked at her like that but she wanted to clear everything up.

'I thought that you were in love with Melanie,' she told him simply.

'No!' His shock was evident and she smiled as the last tiny doubt flew away.

'Yes!' she teased. 'It's obvious how much you care about her and Jamie, too, so it just seemed to all add up.'

'All I can say is that obviously maths isn't your strong point!' he declared fiercely. He suddenly sighed and ran a gentle finger down her cheek. 'Did you honestly believe that, Karen?'

When she nodded he drew her closer, holding her so tightly that she could feel the tremor which worked its way through his body.

'You must have felt so confused. No wonder you reacted the way you did. I love Melanie as a sister and I care what happens to her and Jamie, but there's no more to it than that. I am not in love with her, which is probably a good job as Hugh would have my guts for garters!'

Karen laughed softly. 'So Denise was right. She mentioned something about Hugh being crazy about Melanie. How does she feel about him, though?'

'Let's just say that I'm hopeful they will get their act together. I think she's finally seeing the light because of how concerned Hugh was about Jamie.'

Karen gasped. 'So it was Hugh she was referring to at the party when she said something about Jamie having been in the safest hands.'

'Probably,' he agreed, then smiled knowingly. 'Ah, you thought she meant me, did you?'

'Uh-huh,' she mumbled. 'Seems that I completely misread the situation, didn't I?' She broke off and stared at him. 'That night I was here when we went up to the tree-house and you...you kissed me.'

'Oh, I remember,' he said in the sort of voice which made her feel as though she were going to melt. She struggled to hold onto her composure a little longer, although it wasn't easy.

'You said something about it being better if we stopped because it wasn't right if we carried on kissing and...and everything,' she muttered, flushing as she saw his amusement.

'And everything? Mmm, that's one way of describing it, I suppose.'

He kissed her hard, his lips drawing an immediate response from her. He sighed as he drew back with obvious reluctance. 'Where was I now...? Ah, yes, in the tree-house. That was me trying to be very sensible that night. It wasn't easy when what I really wanted to do was carry you straight off to my bed and make mad, passionate love to you. However, I sensed that although you seemed willing you weren't ready for that kind of commitment at that stage.'

He turned her so that he could look straight into her eyes. 'I needed to know that you trusted me, Karen, that you knew I wouldn't let you down like you'd been let down before. I didn't want to use the attraction we felt for one another to influence you in any way in case you regretted it later.'

'And I thought you stopped because of Melanie, because you were too honourable to make love to one woman when you were in love with another.'

'No wonder you behaved so oddly and avoided me afterwards!' Nick groaned as he pulled her into his arms and held her so that she could feel his heart beating against her.

'It was the only way I could handle the situation.' She drew back and glared at him. 'Anyway, if we're talking about odd behaviour, then how about the way you behaved in the canteen this lunch-time? You virtually told me that you couldn't care less if I was seeing someone else!'

'Lies, all lies! Inside I was eaten up with jealousy, my sweet. Why do you think I left without eating my lunch?' he admitted ruefully. 'I knew that if I stayed I'd end up giving you the third degree about who this fellow was who had taken you away from me!'

'And I thought you couldn't care less!' She smiled at him, her heart in her eyes. 'There isn't anyone else, Nick. It's you and only you I love.'

'And it's you *I* love, Karen. You I want to spend the rest of my life with, if you'll have me?'

'Mmm, I'm not sure.'

Funny how at this most important moment in her life she found the ability to tease him. Maybe it was knowing that Nick was as crazy about her as she was about him which gave her the confidence. Or maybe it was because she knew that he trusted her not to hurt him. Trust was a two-way street; it needed to be received as well as given.

She stood up and held out her hand, smiling when he immediately got up and took it. 'Maybe I need just a little *persuasion!*'

Nick swept her into his arms and kissed her hard. His eyes were alight with love and laughter as he looked at her. 'Then you've come to the right man. Trust me, Karen, I'll soon help you make up your mind!'

Karen kissed him back. 'Of course I trust you, Nick. There's no question about that!'

'Good. However, there is one proviso. I hope you'll understand why I want to do this, sweetheart.'

'What is it, Nick?' she asked, wondering why he sounded so serious all of a sudden.

'I want our wedding night to be the first time we sleep together. I know it sounds crazy in this day and age but it's something I really and truly believe is the right thing for us to do.'

She stared at him in bewilderment, not sure that she understood. 'But why do you want us to wait, Nick?' She blushed and looked away. 'You know I want you and I think that you want me.'

'More than anything in the world! I want to hold you in my arms and make love to you, go to sleep knowing that you'll be there beside me in the morning.'

He kissed her tenderly, his eyes adoring her. 'I want to spend every day of my life with you beside me, but when we sleep together for the very first time I want it to be really special. I want you to be absolutely sure that I want you for who you are, not just what you can give me. I want it to be the most magical, wonderful night of your life.'

'Oh, Nick. I love you so much. And, yes, if that's what you want, then it's what I want too.' She kissed him lovingly, then cupped his face between her hands. 'Our wedding night will be a night to cherish for the rest of our lives, won't it?'

'It will, although there are going to be an awful lot of wonderful nights to remember, my darling. Every night we have together is going to be so special.'

Nick pulled her to him and the kiss they shared was all the more wonderful because it was just a forerunner of what was to come. Karen twined her arms around his neck and held him tight, knowing that she was the luckiest woman in the world to have found a love like this and a man she could trust for ever.

EPILOGUE

'How do the Seychelles sound to you?'

Karen looked up as Nick popped his head round the door. She hadn't expected to see him until lunch-time so this unexpected visit was all the more welcome. Funny how much she missed him when they were apart even for a couple of hours.

Now she smiled as he came and perched on the edge of her desk. 'Hot is the word that springs to mind.' She glanced towards the window and grimaced. 'However, that is a definite plus factor with weather like this. I just hope that it stops raining in time for the wedding!'

'It won't make a scrap of difference if it buckets it down!' Nick leant over and kissed her soundly. He grinned as he saw her dreamy expression. 'Good. The magic hasn't worn off yet, I see.'

'Smug devil!' she retorted, smiling at him. She sighed. 'And you're right because I don't care if it hails, rains or snows so long as we get married. Just think, only three weeks to go now.'

'And then you will be Mrs Bentley. I'm counting the days!' He stood up and pulled a travel brochure out of his pocket. 'Hugh gave me this. Considering how that man has hung about all these months, he certainly knows how to get things moving!'

Karen laughed. Hugh and Melanie had announced their engagement two days after she and Nick had told everyone that they were getting married. It had caused a great deal of amusement and both men had come in for a lot of rib-

183

bing from the rest of the staff. As Denise had put it dryly, there had to be something in the air!

If there was, then it should be bottled and sold, Karen thought, picking up the brochure. It certainly didn't seem fair that others shouldn't feel as happy as she did!

'It looks lovely, Nick,' she said, glancing at the pictures of sunlit tropical beaches. So far everything had gone so perfectly to plan that it was a little scary at times. She'd bought her dress—creamy duchesse satin with tiny pearls encrusting the bodice—and they'd booked the church in the village where she had been born, then arranged to hold the reception at a hotel nearby.

Nick had been a huge hit with her family as well when she had taken him to meet them. He had insisted on formally asking her father for permission to marry her and charmed her mother. He'd even met her brother, home for the weekend from university, and gained that young man's respect by giving him tips on how to make the best of his social life! Now there was just the honeymoon to sort out, but funnily enough they couldn't seem to decide where they wanted to go. Maybe it was the fact that it was so important that they found the perfect place for their first night which made it so hard to decide.

'It does look lovely,' Karen agreed.

'But?' Nick laughed. 'There was a definite *but* in there, sweetheart.'

'I know. It's so funny but I can't seem to make up my mind where I want to go.' She closed the brochure. 'You decide, Nick. Surprise me.'

'Well, if you're sure you trust me enough to choose the right place?' he queried.

'You know I do,' she said softly, smiling at him with her heart in her eyes. It earned her another kiss before Nick—very reluctantly—got up to leave.

'Time I did some work. Oh, I saw Kevin on my way in. He was telling me that he'd spent the weekend with Ian's parents.'

'Yes. He was so excited about it too.' Her face clouded for a moment. 'It was so sad about Ian dying like that, wasn't it? I really feel for his parents.'

'It must be hard for them, but I imagine it helps to know that those last few weeks of Ian's life were so happy. That was mainly thanks to you introducing the two boys, Karen.'

'I'm so glad it worked out so well. The support Kevin is receiving from Ian's parents has made a world of difference to him and I believe that his school has nominated him for a Good Citizen Award because of his visits to Ian. His father told me the last time he brought Kevin in and he even sounded pleased!'

'Miracle of miracles!' Nick replied ruefully. 'Right, I'll have to run. See you later. You're sure about this?'

He tapped the brochure and Karen nodded. 'Quite sure. You choose where we go, Nick. It's going to be wonderful wherever it is, so I don't care where you decide on.'

'I hope you mean that,' he said thoughtfully, turning towards the door. Karen frowned as he left, wondering what he had thought of. He'd definitely thought of something from the look on his face.

She smiled to herself as she went to fetch Kevin in. She trusted Nick enough to know that it would be perfect whatever he chose, so she wasn't going to worry.

It had been the most wonderful day. Not even the weather—rain *and* snow!—had marred her enjoyment of it. Marrying Nick was simply the culmination of all her dreams and as she had taken her vows in the tiny village church where she had been christened Karen had meant every word. For better for worse. For richer for poorer. In sickness and in health. Her love for Nick and his for her wouldn't be dimmed by any of those things.

'Almost there.'

She glanced round and smiled at him, thinking how handsome he looked in his formal suit. He had whisked her away from the reception and into the car after giving her barely enough time to change out of her wedding dress. She still had no idea where they were going for their honeymoon but she hadn't asked. However, it was a bit of a surprise when they pulled up in front of Nick's house in London a short time later.

'Was there a problem with the flights?' she queried as he got out to open her door.

'No.' He helped her from the car, smiling as he saw her bewilderment. 'Everything has been arranged, sweetheart. You'll see.'

He led her straight through the house to the kitchen and unlocked the door, then turned to her. 'You said that you wanted a surprise so I hope you aren't disappointed.'

Karen had no idea what he meant. She followed him into the garden and gasped. Turning in a slow circle, she tried to take in the sight which met her but it was hard to believe what she was seeing. Every tree and bush was strung with tiny white lights so that the garden looked like a fairy glen. That was stunning enough, but when she looked up she suddenly realised there was more to come.

Dazedly she let Nick lead her to the tree-house, then just stood gazing upwards. 'How…?' She gulped. 'I mean, we were in Yorkshire so who did all this?'

'Hugh, Melanie and Jamie. Remember they said that they had to leave early?' Nick kissed her softly on the mouth. 'I told Hugh exactly what I wanted doing and, like the good friend he is, he came haring back here. I hope you like it, darling. Come and see.'

He led the way up the ladder, waiting to help her at the top. Karen stepped inside the tiny cabin and looked round in amazement. Every shelf and surface held a white candle and the soft light they gave out created a magical atmosphere. The cabin was deliciously warm as well, thanks to the heat flowing from an electric heater which had been fitted to one of the walls.

'I had an electrician run a cable from the house,' Nick explained. He laughed softly. 'He thought I was mad, quite frankly, said he'd never been asked to wire a tree-house before and especially not at this time of the year!'

He closed the cabin door, then turned to her with a hint of uncertainty in his eyes. 'Do you think I'm mad to expect you to like this, Karen? If it's any consolation, then I have plane tickets in my pocket for tomorrow...'

She stopped him the most effective way she knew, her lips clinging to his as her heart overflowed. That he should have gone to so much trouble to make this night special for her was proof she didn't need of how much he loved her!

'It's perfect, Nick. I couldn't have wished for anything more wonderful than this. I love you so much.'

'And I love you too.'

A sudden squall of wind hit the cabin and some of the candles went out. Neither of them noticed. They were too busy creating a magic all of their own.

0110 Gen Std HB

MILLS & BOON®

FEBRUARY 2010 HARDBACK TITLES

ROMANCE

At the Boss's Beck and Call	Anna Cleary
Hot-Shot Tycoon, Indecent Proposal	Heidi Rice
Revealed: A Prince and A Pregnancy	Kelly Hunter
Hot Boss, Wicked Nights	Anne Oliver
The Millionaire's Misbehaving Mistress	Kimberly Lang
Between the Italian's Sheets	Natalie Anderson
Naughty Nights in the Millionaire's Mansion	Robyn Grady
Sheikh Boss, Hot Desert Nights	Susan Stephens
Bought: One Damsel in Distress	Lucy King
The Billionaire's Bought Mistress	Annie West
Playboy Boss, Pregnancy of Passion	Kate Hardy
A Night with the Society Playboy	Ally Blake
One Night with the Rebel Billionaire	Trish Wylie
Two Weeks in the Magnate's Bed	Nicola Marsh
Magnate's Mistress…Accidentally Pregnant	Kimberly Lang
Desert Prince, Blackmailed Bride	Kim Lawrence
The Nurse's Baby Miracle	Janice Lynn
Second Lover	Gill Sanderson

HISTORICAL

The Rake and the Heiress	Marguerite Kaye
Wicked Captain, Wayward Wife	Sarah Mallory
The Pirate's Willing Captive	Anne Herries

MEDICAL™

Angel's Christmas	Caroline Anderson
Someone To Trust	Jennifer Taylor
Morrison's Magic	Abigail Gordon
Wedding Bells	Meredith Webber

MILLS & BOON

FEBRUARY 2010 LARGE PRINT TITLES

ROMANCE

Desert Prince, Bride of Innocence	Lynne Graham
Raffaele: Taming His Tempestuous Virgin	Sandra Marton
The Italian Billionaire's Secretary Mistress	Sharon Kendrick
Bride, Bought and Paid For	Helen Bianchin
Betrothed: To the People's Prince	Marion Lennox
The Bridesmaid's Baby	Barbara Hannay
The Greek's Long-Lost Son	Rebecca Winters
His Housekeeper Bride	Melissa James

HISTORICAL

The Brigadier's Daughter	Catherine March
The Wicked Baron	Sarah Mallory
His Runaway Maiden	June Francis

MEDICAL™

Emergency: Wife Lost and Found	Carol Marinelli
A Special Kind of Family	Marion Lennox
Hot-Shot Surgeon, Cinderella Bride	Alison Roberts
A Summer Wedding at Willowmere	Abigail Gordon
Miracle: Twin Babies	Fiona Lowe
The Playboy Doctor Claims His Bride	Janice Lynn

0210 Gen Std HB

MILLS & BOON®

MARCH 2010 HARDBACK TITLES

ROMANCE

Greek Tycoon, Inexperienced Mistress	Lynne Graham
The Master's Mistress	Carole Mortimer
The Andreou Marriage Arrangement	Helen Bianchin
Untamed Italian, Blackmailed Innocent	Jacqueline Baird
Bought: Destitute yet Defiant	Sarah Morgan
Wedlocked: Banished Sheikh, Untouched Queen	Carol Marinelli
The Virgin's Secret	Abby Green
The Prince's Royal Concubine	Lynn Raye Harris
Married Again to the Millionaire	Margaret Mayo
Claiming His Wedding Night	Lee Wilkinson
Outback Bachelor	Margaret Way
The Cattleman's Adopted Family	Barbara Hannay
Oh-So-Sensible Secretary	Jessica Hart
Housekeeper's Happy-Ever-After	Fiona Harper
Sheriff Needs a Nanny	Teresa Carpenter
Sheikh in the City	Jackie Braun
The Doctor's Lost-and-Found Bride	Kate Hardy
Desert King, Doctor Daddy	Meredith Webber

HISTORICAL

The Viscount's Unconventional Bride	Mary Nichols
Compromising Miss Milton	Michelle Styles
Forbidden Lady	Anne Herries

MEDICAL™

Miracle: Marriage Reunited	Anne Fraser
A Mother for Matilda	Amy Andrews
The Boss and Nurse Albright	Lynne Marshall
New Surgeon at Ashvale A&E	Joanna Neil